ALAN E. LONGWORTH

I Never saw My Father Smile

TRAFFORD

Note for Librarians: A cataloguing record for this book is available from Library and
Archives Canada at www.collectionscanada.ca/amicus/index-e.html
ISBN 1-4251-1317-6

*Printed in Victoria, BC, Canada. Printed on paper with minimum 30% recycled fibre.
Trafford's print shop runs on "green energy" from solar, wind and other environmentally-
friendly power sources.*

Offices in Canada, USA, Ireland and UK

Book sales for North America and international:
Trafford Publishing, 6E–2333 Government St.,
Victoria, BC V8T 4P4 CANADA
phone 250 383 6864 (toll-free 1 888 232 4444)
fax 250 383 6804; email to orders@trafford.com
Book sales in Europe:
Trafford Publishing (UK) Limited, 9 Park End Street, 2nd Floor
Oxford, UK OX1 1HH UNITED KINGDOM
phone +44 (0)1865 722 113 (local rate 0845 230 9601)
facsimile +44 (0)1865 722 868; info.uk@trafford.com
Order online at:
trafford.com/06-3076

10 9 8 7 6 5 4 3 2

CHAPTER ONE.

With unleashed anger that had lain dormant within my breast until this moment. I grabbed the carving knife from the counter and plunged it deep into my father's chest. I used all the power my arm could muster exactly the way the military had taught me how to kill during my basic training. Jerking back the knife, I re-deployed it, sinking it up to the hilt under his ribs on his right side. Father began to sink down to his knees. With my anger now bordering on uncontrolled madness I thrust the knife over and over into his vile body as my father wide eyed in surprise and agony, moaned and dropped to the floor. A grimace, or was it a glimmer of a smile crossed his rat like face. I can never be sure now which, but at that moment I perceived it to be an evil smile following the grin of righteous superiority over me that had precipitated my burst of violence upon his person.

His was the ultimate insult, sending me over the edge of sanity. I took the knife and bent over him slashing his throat from ear to ear. Our farm kitchen resembled an abattoir-killing floor as his blood flowed onto it with him spreading it all over the linoleum in his death throes. As he lay looking up at me with his life quickly ebbing, I spit right into his dying eyes. I knew that from this point on my father could no longer hurt me and I began to regain my sanity and composure. I stood over his offensive body watching detached and calm until death took him. Now we were both free and I remembered that from my earliest memories that I never saw my father smile.

It has been a number of years since I slaughtered him like he was a butcher hog. Not that I have any regrets, I don't, but the memory of that day are as fresh in my mind as if it were just yesterday.

My father, Jed Branson, had entered the world squawking and kicking in the back bedroom of the Branson farmhouse, forty-five years before I dispatched him unceremoniously into the next world in the kitchen of the same house. As I sit here alone within these four narrow walls, with all the time in the world to think about it. I can see him quite clear in my minds eye, just as if were sitting in front of me right now at this moment in his usual place by the wood burning stove. Father always dressed in farm type overalls which he generally referred to as overhauls. He wore one of those rough collarless shirts that the farm folks in Gage County all did in those days. In the shirt's left pocket a can of Skol chewing tobacco bulged out within easy reach of his grasping stained fingers.

Father had two pairs of high work boots. The best pair polished for Sunday church wear, the others worn for the farm work often were coated in Gage County's rich mud. Mother's pleadings that he either clean them or take them off before coming into the house leaving mud tracks on the linoleum, went unheeded as did all her other requests of him.

My father had a mean narrow face with eyes bulging from under slits of eyelids. They reminded me of the faces of the rats that we often found in the bean silos. Outdoors, he wore a battered wide brimmed hat stained with the sweat of many seasons, the brim, shading his rodent like eyes from the Gage County sun. My father's teeth and cruel pursed lips were coated in a foul appearing brown tobacco juice. His habit of spitting his tobacco juice into the fire grate of the kitchen stove infuriated my mother and created a feeling of repugnance in me. When not wearing his hat, wispy auburn hair hung in sweat tangled strings which mother trimmed for him with the kitchen shears while he preached at her from his tattered bible. The kitchen of the Branson farmhouse had seen neither a coat of paint nor any other upgrading since grandfather's day.

My grandfather also began his life at the Branson farmhouse. It had built in the late eighteen hundreds by my great grandfather, Josiah Branson. Josiah had come to Gage County from the southern states where he had a strict religious upbringing. Farmland was dirt cheap in those days and Gage County was beginning to get a reputation for growing high quality beans. 'Something in the soil they said.'

Josiah had brought with him a mousy little wife, obedient to her husband and well and truly indoctrinated in the subservient role of a woman, as dictated by the Southern Baptist religion. Martha Branson bore two sons. Both she and Josiah pushed their religious beliefs constantly at the boys, Ezekiel and Abraham. The two boys were considered no better than chattels and expected to give unlimited free labor to Josiah and Martha. At age sixteen, Ezekiel the oldest, rebelled at the constant hard farm labor and the strident teachings of his parents. Consequently, one July night he crept from the farmhouse walking away through the farm gate never to return or contact his family. With brother Ezekiel out of the picture an extra workload was placed on the shoulders of young Abraham.

Abe, as they commonly called him, reached young adulthood, browbeaten, indoctrinated in bible matters and having no ambition or hope for a life of his own. His existence consisted of a mundane routine of plowing, planting, harvesting and spending countless hours on his knees in prayer. When his father, Josiah succumbed to pneumonia just after Abe's twenty-fourth birthday. Abe, ill prepared to run the farm, took to embracing his religion with a fierce un-natural fervor. Uneducated in dealing with others in a reasonable manner, Abe began ordering his mother about treating her like a no account heathen and working her as though she were no better than a stubborn mule deserving of the whip.

Martha Branson, suffering the ravages of advancing age and overwork, died alone in a bean field still clutching a hoe in her hands. Now alone with a house to run and crops to plant and harvest, Abe knew he had to have help. He began to make inquiries at his church, resulting in him being introduced to a woman a few years older than he. Winifred Montcalm had been left a widow, with her husband having made no financial provisions for her. In desperate need of a home and sustenance she

4

readily agreed to marry Abe Branson. Not having the same religious fervor as he, friction in the Branson house began the first day of her arrival and soon escalated to the point of them hating each other.

Abe forced his marital rights upon the protesting Winifred and as a result of what she considered to be rape, she bore Abe, a shrew-like son. Her husband named him Jeddadiah. Winifred Branson didn't love her unwanted child. In fact she barely tolerated him believing the boy to be as foul as the one who had so callously spawned him. As a result, Jeddadiah grew into a morose boy often punished, always worked hard and constantly bombarded with lectures of Hell fire and brimstone from his father and complete indifference from his mother.

A walk to the church twice each Sunday for worship was the only time, Jed as he became to be known, ever left the Branson bean farm. As a result he never developed any social skills or interests other than prayer, bible reading and bean farming. He knew little of the world outside the farm gate, nor did he care to. As far as he was concerned only the people to be associated with were the congregation of his church. All others were classified in his mind as heathens fit only to be shunned, destined for the Devil's pit.

In mid life, Abe developed a severe type of arthritis. As a result, the job of running the Branson farm fell upon the shoulders of Jed and his mother, while Abe, unwilling to give up any kind of control gave them work orders from his high-backed chair by the stove.

The Gage County Bean Co-op kept the price of dried beans artificially low, consequently after the farm essentials were dealt with, no money remained for any kind of luxuries. The Branson's lived in a house bereft of laughter, music, or joy resulting in the occupants living suspended in a state of constant sustained misery.

At the age of twenty-two, my father, Jed brought Hattie his new wife to live at the farm. Hattie Margerson came from a farm family of six daughters. Like her sisters, Hattie had been brought up to know hard farm labor and had calluses on her hands from working in the bean fields with her parents to prove it. The Margerson family attended the same church as my family, but they had a much more liberal view of religion. Eight mouths to feed on the proceeds of the Margerson bean crop stretched their financial resources to the limit. The impending marriage between, Hattie and Jed Branson came as good news to her cash-strapped parents. They may have had an inkling of the Branson family history, but if they did, they kept it to themselves and encouraged the union.

I do not think for one minute my mother had any idea what she was stepping into by marrying Jed Branson. She came as a new farm bride into a household poisoned with the most appalling social conditions. I recall her once telling me that she knew of father's strong religious views before they were married and while reluctant, she prepared to live with them. However she had not counted on living with a bible-thumping fanatic, along with his rude, ignorant and equally uncompromising father together with his sour, downtrodden and silent slave-like wife.

My mother right up to the end of her life wore cheap cotton dresses she bought through the Sears Roebuck catalogue. On her feet she wore unladylike sturdy work boots with white socks rolled down to just above the boot tops. On her head she wore a frilly cotton cap to keep the bean dust out of her hair. I have no recollection of her wearing makeup of any kind. I would imagine my father would have gone on a wild verbal and physical rampage had he found her wearing lip rouge. He held the opinion that only scarlet women painted themselves in the colours of harlots. I remember my mother as having a pleasant face although not a spectacular beauty, but when she and I were alone her smile offered some brightness to my shadowed world. Her smiles were reserved for me in private, for having lived so long with my father she had ceased to smile at anything. She told me once that not even on her wedding day, 'I never saw your father smile.'

Mother never really said much about her relationship with father, but even in my young mind I was convinced the marriage from her point of view was one of resigned desperation. Some nights I heard them having terrible arguments from down below my room, mostly about money, or more likely the lack of it. From the snippets of the heated conversations I heard, father was adamant that the church tithe was vital to our family being brought to the gates of heaven. It was his opinion and one that was forced upon us all, that managing without worldly goods and enduring hard labour and suffering, better prepared us to meet God.

I first saw the light of day in the back bedroom of the Branson farmhouse. I gathered from mother in later years, that I was not particularly welcomed into the Branson snake pit of a home. Grandfather Branson complained long and bitterly about my crying, yelling at mother to shut the little brat up, while my Grandmother moaned constantly about the extra washing she had to do, also whining about the fact that more of the farm work had been piled on her during the final weeks of mother's pregnancy.

I had reached the age of three years when my Grandfather died in his sleep. After the funeral, Grandmother Branson announced that now she was free of the old tyrant she would be treated like a Clydesdale horse no longer. She would depart this awful place of hard labor and misdirected piety; she would go this very day to live with her sister over in Harrison County.

Before the Gage County's rich soil had settled atop Grandfather's grave, Winifred Branson, with her shoulders erect for the first time in years and the hint of a smile reflecting a newfound freedom on her lips, walked determinedly out of the Branson farmhouse. Carrying a canvas bag containing her meagre belongings she did not look back but strode away never to return, or communicate with my parents ever again.

It seems odd now as I look back, I never missed my Grandmother. I can only assume that she felt as little for me as she did for her unwanted son. I have no recollection of her ever offering a kind word or affection to me, not even after one of my father's punishments. It was so long ago and I so very young have not even a vague memory of what I may have done wrong at the time, but I do remember the pain of my father's renditions of.

'Spare the rod and spoil the child.'

Mother never intervened in my father's violent acts against me. She would leave the house, I presume because she could not bear to watch the biblical justice he meted out. Having had an abundant amount of time in the intervening years to consider my father's actions, I think he must have gained a warped sense of power over the household that precluded any acts of rebellion from my mother. When father's punishments were meted out and he had left the room or house, mother would attempt to comfort me. It is my opinion that my mother passed on to me her quiet acceptance of things we were powerless to change, along with her yellowy blonde hair and deep blue eyes that were all to often clouded with sadness and un-shed tears.

I always knew that my mother loved me, her actions proved it, but for fear of my father's vile temper and intolerance, she dared not display fondness toward me in front of him. There were times when she would buy me a small gift at the bean co-op General Store; out of the barely adequate housekeeping money she was allotted. I recall how she always made the presentation to me when father was absent, knowing his aversion to what he termed 'worldly goods.' Father's financial world consisted of a subsistence level of staples for the house, sufficient cash for seed, fertilizer and tithe money for the church. Speaking of which, I could never understand why all we farm folks lived in abject poverty, while our Pastor lived in a large brick house and bought a new Buick car every second year. Father claimed it was because the Pastor was a man of God. 'As ye give, so shall ye receive,' he would say.

Mother had a multiple role at the Branson farm. Not only did she have housework duties, she worked in the fields alongside her husband during the planting and harvesting seasons. Also at the busy canning period at the bean co-op, she worked in the plant helping to make tons of baked beans along with tomatoes trucked in from Harrison County, molasses from Louisiana and condiments shipped in from Chicago. Some days she worked in the shipping department, lifting cases of twenty-four cans of baked beans. She would come home utterly exhausted on those days. But father still ordered her to prepare the evening meal, tidy the house and work with a hoe in the fields until dark. As if that were not enough, she had to join him on her knees for an hour in evening prayer.

When the canning had all been completed with the last of the tomato crop for the season, mother stood all day at a bagging machine, weighing and bagging one-pound bags of dried beans for the retail market. She received minimum wages for her labor, but it made a world of difference to the general revenue of the Branson farm. The larger portion of the farm income went right back into the coffers of the Gage County Bean Co-op for seed beans, fertilizer and the bulk of the family groceries purchased at the co-op general store. Mother, on top of all this managed to maintain a large kitchen garden where she produced potatoes, beets, cabbage, onions and peas. For her own miniscule pleasure she grew a few flowers. My father's only contribution to the kitchen garden was to plow it for her each spring with the tractor.

"It's woman's work," I often heard him declare. I believe that father thought that keeping my mother always busy brought her closer to Godliness since it gave her no time to stray from the straight and narrow.

The Branson farm kept a couple of dozen or so chickens in a small shed beyond the bean silos. The general practice being when the chickens stopped producing eggs for the house, they were summarily slaughtered for the cooking pot. The job of feeding the birds a mixture of ground beans with vegetable peelings and collecting the eggs fell to me at an early age. Father always did the killing, while mother had to eviscerate and pluck the feathers from the unfortunate bird. We raised a pig for our own use every year, they thrived gorging on the bean straw and were ready to butcher in October most years.

Father did the butchering, assisted by mother and I. To see him take the life of the screaming and struggling animal with his long knife, as mother and I held it down used to terrify me. I felt nauseated as we scalded the animal's skin and scraped off the wiry hair. Father then hung the carcass by the back legs and gutted it. I often puked at the smell of the steaming pile of intestines on the ground. While mocking my fragile stomach, Father would make me pick up the kidneys and liver and put them in large bowls. I always dreaded slaughter day and felt that my father enjoyed both the killing and making sport of my weaker sensibilities.

'This will be your job one day boy! Get used to it,' he would shout into my ear through his dark brown teeth.

At the age of six, mother dispatched me to school. It wasn't a real school, our Gage County rural area didn't have one, but a group of local farm kids met in Mrs. Bartoski's parlour. Mrs. Bartoski was as different as chalk and cheese from my parents. She was kind and seemed to have the children's interests at heart. She never punished us if we did our work incorrectly, instead she explained gently and thoroughly the right way to do it. I loved school. At last I had others my age to converse and to play with outside during the breaks. I knew that Mrs. Bartoski went to the same church as my family, but never once did I hear her pushing her religious views upon us. She taught us something of the world outside Gage County for most of us had no knowledge of the world beyond our farm gates. As I remember now, she was not highly educated herself but she did impart to her students some primitive groundwork in Math, Geography and American History. Under her tutelage we learned how to get by in reading and writing.

I suppose, thinking back on it I began to lead an odd kind of double life, as a survival tactic I developed a dual personality. At school I was happy and outgoing; I enjoyed learning and the company of the other farm kids. Here there was no peer pressure about the way I dressed; for most of the other boys wore their father's worn out hand-me-down overalls with the legs cut off short and the excess materiel used for patching. The overalls were so large on us kids that there was room inside them for two boys and they hung from our shoulders like bean sacks. Our shirts too were hand-me-downs, so large draped on our small bodies that they hid the fact that we had no underwear. Some of the boys had boots that fit them but the greater part of us wore our father's oversize old ones, or came to school barefoot. Despite the way we youngsters were dressed, we never felt we were poor. We were the children of bean farmers and this was how life was for us. So far as we knew, this is how things were all over America.

On arrival back at the farm, I had to leave my cloak of outgoing and happy attitude at the gate and wear a different mantle of misery and blind obedience.

Throughout my early years, I never saw my father smile. He would look at me when I walked through the farm gate from school. I could read scorn in his eyes as I approached in clothing ten sizes to large for my young body. In retrospect I suppose I must have looked quite odd, but it was not of my doing. I respected my father. Yes I feared him, but I did respect him. After all he was my father, the head of the Branson family. I could never figure out if he had any real feelings for me, if he hated me, or just despised me for reasons I knew nothing of. He never verbalized his true feelings leaving me to believe he thought of me as just another form of farm livestock, to do his bidding without question.

Such was my early childhood. When I reached age seven, father felt it was time I was earning my keep. Now there were chores for me to complete before and after school. On weekends I worked in the fields alongside my mother. She would help me with tasks that were too hard for me to do alone. Sometimes I would pick her a bunch of wildflowers from along the creek. She always greeted my gift with a smile, at other times with a kiss and it pleased me to know I had pleased her.

In my enthusiasm I picked some for my father. He gazed at me with a look of derision in his mean eyes, threw the flowers down and crushed them under his booted heel.

"Have you no work to do boy? God does not suffer idle hands," he said in a cruel and menacing voice. His hand darted out and slapped my cheek. I forced back the tears that fought valiantly to cascade down my cheeks.

"Yes Sir," I answered. I went back to my hoe and when my back was to him, I let the tears flood forth. It was not the slap causing my distress, I was used to that. It was his rejection of my gesture of my hesitant affection, the first of many to cut me to the core over time. I must have been a resilient child, for I never ceased trying and despite my best efforts to please him, the results were always the same. I never saw my father smile.

With each bean-growing season, like the beans, I grew taller and stronger and my workload increased accordingly. When I reached the age of eleven years, I first noticed how my mother coughed so brutishly hard and long, especially after the bean threshing. I don't know much about medical matters even now, but I think she was allergic to the black dust that flew off the dried bean pods in voluminous clouds at threshing time.

Since threshing was very much a family affair, for several days mother was always in the thick of the dust cloud. At this late date I am convinced that the dust filled her lungs and was slowly killing her. Her cough was so extended and arduous I could swear that she came close to coughing up her guts. The rebellion in her lungs went on not for days, but for up to two months, in which she got very little sleep. Yet my father continued to work her like a plow horse. I remember the year that mother bought me a whittling knife at the bean co-op General Store. It became my most-prized possession. It seemed to give me a new lease on life. After chores were done for the day, I would sit by the kitchen stove and whittle wooden carvings of small animals and birds.

Not to brag, but I became quite good at it. Mother would complement me on my skill and say to father,

"See what Clem has made. Isn't he clever?" He would raise his eyes from the bible look at my work with a face that reeked of silent sarcasm, then go back to his bible. Occasionally I would present father with one of my carvings, he would hold it in his hand and look at it and promptly toss it into the stove firebox. Of course I would be disappointed that he thought so little of my efforts to even comment. However I had become accustomed to his indifference to my feelings since it was almost a daily occurrence. Mother's cough did not get much better the year I turned twelve. I think she may have known her time on earth was limited, for on my birthday she presented me with an inexpensive wood carving kit. I have always believed that mother scrimped and saved for it in order that I should have something to remember her by and indeed if that were her purpose she succeeded. For I think of her each time I run my hands over the smooth wooden box. It was shortly afterwards that her coughing began to produce black blood clots, within a matter of hours mother coughed her last and fell into the dirt between two heaped rows of plants in the garden expiring unattended clutching a pail of potatoes.

My life changed on that dreadful day. No longer could I expect any warmth or affection in my young existence. I could look forward only to misery, hard labor and increased religious rhetoric from the mean narrow mouth of my father. Father had ensured with his morose attitude that our family had no close friends to help send mother on her celestial way. With few mourners in attendance, Mother's body was interred at the church graveyard. I do not believe my father mourned her. Instead I sensed anger in him at the loss of her income from the bean co-op, along with the loss of her labor for the farm and the house.

15

"Boy! It is God's will that you should take over the duties of running the house and assisting in the fields. There will be no more time wasted on schooling for you; it is of no value to God, nor to me."

My father's words struck me like a poleaxe. I expected such an edict of course but I felt he could have first let me grieve my mother for a few days, instead of dumping his proclamation onto my shoulders before we had even left the graveyard.

I remember going to see the schoolteacher, Mrs. Bartoski to give her the news.

"You will be missed, Clem. You have been doing so well with your lessons. It seems a shame that you cannot continue, perhaps if you ask your father again he will allow you to keep up with your education."

Mrs. Bartoski's words almost choked me. I didn't need to ask to know my father's vitriolic answer. But because she had encouraged me, I did ask. For my question I reaped the full volume of his wrath. I received three lashes from his belt and a lengthy venomous tirade about my duty to God and parent. As I gazed at his angry face with reluctant tears clouding my vision, it occurred to me once again that thus far in my life, I never saw my father smile.

Despite my young age and inexperience, I was expected to produce three meals per day for the two of us. Most of the time I did all right but a failure or an accidental burning of our meal would net me a heavy slap about my ears and a lecture on wasting the food given us by the Lord. I had to attend to laundry, bed making and house cleaning as well as a full day's labor in the bean fields.

16

Most days for me now meant a dull round of work, sleep, loneliness and boredom. On days where the work had been lighter than usual, I would in the evening bring out my carving kit run my fingers over the box and think of my mother. Then I would open it and sit by the stove and create the likeness of some small creature from a piece of kindling while father read his bible and then he would make me kneel and pray with him.

Once I got the idea to carve father a pair of wooden clogs like those ones on the picture on the scouring powder can that the Dutchmen wore. I thought he might like them and wear them around the house. I found two sycamore fireplace logs and began my task. It took me three weeks of evening carving to complete them. I drew a picture of a tulip on each clog toe and colored them with some yellow paint I had found in the tractor shed. Upon presenting them to father he turned them over in his hands then one by one stuffed them into the stove fire and without a single word crossing his lips, went back to reading his bible.

A great loneliness began to affect me. Since my schooling had ended I had never been beyond the farm gate except to accompany father to church. Father went to the co-op in town for the grocery supplies once each week leaving me a list of chores. For weeks on end I saw no one but my father, but he spoke only to pray out loud, give orders, or to chastise me for some perceived wrong. On rare occasions a traveling salesman might come to the farm, but father quickly gave them marching orders. He said he would not have people on his property who were not devout Christians, like himself.

I look back now on those several years after mother's

death and believe that my mind stagnated. Mental stimulation was non-existent, conversation just a distant memory. No books other than the bible were permitted in the Branson house and I had no one I could write to. I lived in real fear of becoming akin to a village idiot. In order to prevent myself becoming like my narrow-minded father, I refused to become obsessed with his religious jargon. To keep myself from becoming completely brain dead I would do math problems on a strip of clean wood with small pieces of charcoal salvaged from the ashes of the kitchen stove. At other times I would close my eyes and try to remember the stories the teacher read to us in school.

Mostly I carved. Several times I made things that I thought father would like but each time he would look at it, then lean forward and pitch it into the stove firebox. Maybe I wasn't too bright at that time, like I said, my brain was becoming stagnated. Despite it, I eventually got his message loud and clear. Father didn't want my gifts. I desperately wanted someone to appreciate my carving. It was some kind of drive where I needed to know that I was a useful and possibly talented human being.

I never left the farm and no one ever came to it. I had never seen any of my schoolmates since my last day there other than at church. Father did not allow me any time to socialize there, for him, church was serious business and if he caught me not paying rapt attention it would net me a savage blow to my ribs with his elbow. After the service we would drive home in complete silence. I would make our lunch after which father spent the afternoon reading the scriptures. Later I would prepare the evening meal then do the evening farm chores.

In the period of time after mother's funeral and before the day I went to apply for my drivers licence, my life resembled being in total darkness twenty-four hours a day. I realize it is an odd statement, by it, I mean that each dawn brought nothing new or bright into my existence. Day melted into night; weeks melted into months, with no sound other than the dull staccato noise of the tractor exhaust, during plowing and harrowing, the squawk of a few chickens and the bare minimum words of instruction from the mean lips of my father. Now, I realize at this juncture of my life that I was utterly starved for human companionship. Other than church services I had not passed through the farm gate for the best part of four years. Had there been a test for it, I believe I would have been declared a fully-fledged village idiot.

"Its time you had a driver's licence. Boy"

My father's words shocked me. This was completely unexpected. My underdeveloped mind ran riot with thoughts of some new kind of freedom. There was the possibility of driving into town with the five-ton bean hauling truck. Maybe the chance to talk to someone my own age, perhaps father would let me deliver the bulk beans to the elevator at the bean co-op. I pictured myself driving the five-ton with the windows cranked down, the wind clean and sharp, rushing through the cab blowing away the cobwebs of loneliness and social bankruptcy shrouding my unused, but eager brain. Could it be that he trusted me sufficiently to purchase the weekly groceries at the co-op General Store? Time would tell. But for now, my excitement reached levels unparalleled.

I had been driving the Allis Chalmers tractor since I had been big enough to be able to reach the clutch pedal;

also I had driven the five-ton in the fields in the lowest gear. I had no qualms about my failing the driver's test; I knew it would be a breeze. Father wordlessly drove the truck to the Motor Vehicles Office parked out front, then led me inside.

"The boy needs a driver's licence," he said placing the five-dollar fee on the counter. The State Government agent wrote down my answers to his questions and then motioned me to go out to the truck with him. I noticed his look of disdain at the state of the cab. Torn seats and mud everywhere, dirty windows and spilled beans underfoot with some of them sprouting new growth. The agent climbed in making sure he didn't get stabbed in the rear end with the broken seat springs. He watched me carefully as I checked the mirrors and pulled out from the curb. We only went a few blocks when he told me to go back to his office.

"You can handle this well enough young fellow. Come inside and I'll issue your licence."

My father sat waiting for me.

"I passed the test Father. I have my drivers licence now," I said excitedly. Not a muscle in his face moved nor did a sound cross his lips. I had hoped for a minimum display of congratulations, perhaps the ultimate compliment a handshake. But without a single word father rose from his chair, walked out to the truck and climbed into the driver's seat. He had succeeded in completely deflating my soaring ego. Even though throughout my life I had grown used to his cold unfeeling behaviour, this event really hurt. I fought back tears that screamed to erupt; I could not let him see how deeply he had wounded me. Had my father let me drive the truck home it would have meant validation of my self worth. But even that was denied me.

The same never-ending round of mindless work in a silent world continued upon returning to the Branson farm. Two weeks later, a load of beans out of our quota had to go to the co-op elevator. Joy of joys, my father told me to take the load in the five-ton. With my load secured and tarped, I pulled out of the farm gate alone for the first time since I had been going to school. It is hard to describe the utter elation I felt, it was an amalgam of freedom newly obtained, a feeling of adventure at moving down a road that led to unknown pleasures and unseen sights. I saw the landscape in a new and wonderful way. Today the trees were greener, the fields were wider and the roadside streams sparkled brighter than I had ever seen them before.

With the cab windows wound completely down, the scented air brought to my nostrils the perfume of a thousand trees and flowers; I heard the captivating song of the moving air titillate my ears. It caressed my face and reminded me of my mother's gentle hand. I felt an amazing sense of power holding the cracked steering wheel in my hands with my foot upon the accelerator controlling this powerful and fast chariot. It reminded me of Mercury, the winged heeled God of ancient times our teacher Mrs Bartoski had spoken of at school. For the first time in my life I had control albeit temporary, of everything around me. I felt complete exhilaration. I wanted to sing out loud. I wanted the birds perched on the fence wires to understand that I knew now the freedom they had always enjoyed. That now I too knew the feeling of fragrant moving air and the sense of soaring suspended by it yet being its master and I like them, a caged bird no longer.

The road to the bean co-op skirted the main highway leading to Twin Rivers. As I drove along, I could see the big highway rigs over the fence speeding along to a multitude of places I could only imagine. The names on the rigs read, New York, Atlanta, Billings Montana and San Diego California. Oh how I envied the freedom those unknown drivers had. Right now at this moment I shared the same liberty as they, but mine would end after unloading the accursed beans then driving back through the Branson farm gate. While they would continue on to some exotic city across America, I would be heading back to abject misery and hard farm labor. I knew it would be much harder for me to endure after today's burst of freedom and the joyous feeling that had buoyed me this far, quickly began to wane.

When I arrived at the packinghouse elevator, I had to wait my turn to unload. Other drivers and bean farmers waited too and stood around chatting. I joined them just to listen to human voices again. Since my father would not allow a radio in the house, I knew nothing of world, state, or current local events, so the talk went over my head most of the time. I think the majority of them knew I was Jed Branson's son after recognizing the decrepit five-ton truck. I could not be sure, but I think they were talking about my father, for every few minutes there would be gales of laughter and the faces all turned to look at me.

The turn of the steering wheel placing me back into the Branson farmyard wrenched at my heart. It was akin to the feeling of kicking out a stool from under my feet with a noose tied firmly around my neck. I wondered how I would be able to continue the life I had been freed of for a few hours. I had sipped and tasted the sweet wine of the world outside the Branson farm gate and I wanted to drink my fill, to bathe myself in its sweetness. I sought to reject the authoritarian and austere life I had known since my earliest memories, but I knew I could not free myself of the shackles of responsibility to my father and the Branson farm.

My father stepped out of the house coming to examine the truck in order to see if I had damaged it in any way. His rat-like eyes peering from his sour face checked all around the vehicle's sun baked fenders. He found nothing amiss so wordlessly handing me a hoe, he pointed to the vegetable garden. I had a distinct sensation of a dungeon door slamming shut, leaving me inside struggling against the darkness of the life of silent servitude to which I had returned.

For reasons he never divulged, father began allowing me to drive the truck each time we were to deliver a load of beans to the elevator. To my complete surprise he also began trusting me to pick up our grocery supplies at the co-op General Store. The interludes driving into town made a huge difference in my life. The misery and drudgery were still the way of existence at the Branson farm but now I had a few glorious hours of freedom each trip to town afforded me.

I imagined myself to be one of those big rig drivers out on the highway. The old and decrepit International five-ton, in my mind became a sleek Freightliner or Mack with high chrome stacks and a mass of wheels burning up the roads of America. I came to believe that being a truck driver was the best thing I could aspire to if I could ever break away from the bondage of the Branson farm. I felt the dream would likely never happen. Father never paid me in money so I did not see how I could ever leave Branson land and enjoy a life of freedom with a modicum of happiness. I had been born the son of a bean farmer, more than likely in time I would become a bean farmer myself, live a life of poverty and sweat and die a bean farmer poor as a church mouse.

Eventually the other drivers at the bean elevator came to know and accept me sometimes they told jokes about women I didn't understand. It made me feel uncomfortable when they did. The only two women I ever really knew were my mother and Mrs. Bartoski my teacher. Since I had never been told anything about women, sex, or love I became acutely embarrassed. It did not seem right to me for them to speak of women in such demeaning terms. I laughed when they laughed, trying desperately to hide my ignorance of the facts of life.

CHAPTER TWO.

The long manila envelope appeared in the mailbox by the farm gate. It bore the name Clem Branson, but father opened it. After his rat like eyes had scanned the contents, he broke his usual silence to rant and rave.

"If the leaders of this country followed God's rules there would be no need for this."

He handed the letter for me to read. It instructed me to report for the military draft. As I said before, I knew little of the world outside the farm. I had no idea what the draft was. As a consequence I did not understand why the letter provoked such anger in my father.

"They can't take you boy! I need you here to work the farm!" he yelled at the top of his voice. It was only when he calmed down to his usual grumpy self, that he grudgingly explained that I had to go into town and give my name to the military, in case they wanted to use me in the army. To be frank I really had little idea what the army was, or did.

Father remained in a state of high agitation for days,

taking out his frustrations out on me in outbursts of verbal abuse. I felt sure I must have done something wrong to be the sole recipient of his wrath. When we went to town to see the draft people, father drove the truck. His face twisted in silent anger with his discolored teeth clenched tightly, making the muscles on his cheeks stand out like hawsers. His mean eyes fixed firmly on the road ahead, never once strayed to note the beauty of the landscape on either side of us, or to speak.

The draft office had been set up in a room adjoining the Motor Vehicle Department. With me trailing close behind him father strode inside. He amazed me by the diatribe that followed,

"My boy Clem has been instructed to report here. He is vital farm labor. He is needed at home. We have a bean crop in the ground and it will need to be harvested shortly. You just might as well forget about this unchristian draft nonsense. If God had wanted people to go and fight wars for governments, he would have ensured it by putting it in the bible. So I'm telling you now, the boy is coming back to the farm with me and that's where he stays!"

The person behind the desk listened to my father's outburst and then cast his eyes to me. I stood before him wearing the most awful hand-me-down patched clothes, oversize boots with no socks and a stained and torn straw hat. I suspect he had never witnessed such a country bumpkin as I in his entire life. His face revealed how he struggled to refrain from bursting into uncontrolled laughter but the smile curling up from his lips gave him away. I may not have been very worldly at that time, but I knew when someone was making light of me. I felt embarrassed, not only at my scarecrow appearance but of my father's immature outburst.

Controlling his inclination to laugh out loud, the clerk asked while looking at me.

"Name please. Do you have your draft notice with you?" As he always had, father spoke on my behalf.

"Have you lost your hearing? You will not need his name Sir. The boy is vital farm labor. He has the Lords work to do on the land."

"Be that as it may Mr. Branson. He still has to register for the draft. It is the law of the land."

"The laws of God are the only ones I believe in, all others are the laws of inferior men. The bible says---"

"Please sit down and be quiet Sir." The clerk interrupted, "I wish to speak to the person instructed to register for our nation's draft."

I could tell that my father was taken aback. I have no recollection of anyone ever before telling him what to do. Pouting, he left the desk and went to sit by the wall. The agent asked my name and a few other questions, typed up a paper and then asked me to sign it.

"That all there is to it young man, you can go back to the farm with your daddy now."

I recognized his last sentence as a veiled insult, however I was used to such taunting so I ignored him and turned to leave. My father seemed surprised they had allowed me to go home; apparently he had been of the opinion that I would be taken immediately to a military camp. It shocked me to realize for the first time in my life that my father didn't know everything about everything.

We picked up our groceries while we were in the vicinity of the bean co-op. I felt mildly disappointed since it meant that I would not enjoy the freedom I felt when I drove the truck in to town alone. I suppose my father felt some kind of relief at me being allowed to come home, for he let me drive. I expected some volatile criticism from the passenger seat but strangely he remained silent until we reached the Branson farmyard.

Inexplicably, I had never noticed before. As I drove in, I looked at our house. For the first time I saw how it looked so run down and decrepit. The porch sagged at the two front corners the posts having bowed from rot at the bases, the rain gutter had cracked open, spilling rainwater onto the porch deck and many of the boards were warped and split. The front door stood almost devoid of any of its original paint the remainder looked cracked and blistered. The casings were burned a deep brown by countless years of baking in the Gage County sun. If they ever had been painted there was no evidence of it. The window frames burned a stark brown, stood out against the once white clapboard walls. The house roof had a three-foot sag from gable to gable, the shingles heavy with living moss. And the chimney bricks sat precariously atop each other in the absence of sufficient mortar. Off to the side of the building, the outhouse leaned in an acute angle, threatening to topple sideways when occupied. Secretly, I hoped that if it ever did, father would be sitting in it and end up in the dung pit that had never been emptied in living memory. The thought caused me to smile to myself. It conjured up a vision of father climbing out of the pit covered in excrement, with his rat-like eyes peering though it and I could well imagine the words issuing from his mouth would not be praising the God he professed to dedicate his life to.

I wondered why the property had been allowed to deteriorate to this point. Could it be that father was just too lazy to make repairs, or was it a result of so much tithe money going to the church, leaving insufficient to buy paint and a bit of new lumber. Having become accustomed to driving into town and seeing the neat tidy homes and gardens there, I wondered why we had to live in such a run down shack not much better than a hog barn.

The bean crop had done well this season; the pods were long and chock full of what would turn out to be top quality beans, provided that the weather remained warm and dry harvesting would be within two or three weeks.

It was then that the next bombshell hit. Another manila envelope arrived in our mailbox. As always, father opened the mail exploding in a fit of anger such as I have never seen. His face, despite the encrusted dirt turned a shade of purple, his eyes bulged out from his skull and his nose flared out like a charging bull.

"I told those people you were vital farm labor!" he shrieked. "I told them we had a crop to bring in! It is Gods will that you be here to help me bring in the harvest. The heathens that are running this country have no concept of Gods plan. It is written, 'as ye sow so shall ye reap.' Have they no knowledge of the scriptures? Do they not understand the seasons of life?"

Father lifted the cast iron skillet from the stove and hurled it across the room. The skillet struck the tabletop, bounced and crashed through the kitchen window. Next he hurled the coffee pot, the salt and peppershakers and a metal container of white flour that struck the kitchen wall clock, breaking it and coating much of the room in

29

a thin layer of flour.

Abruptly, father ceased his tirade, threw the letter onto the table and walked out onto the porch with the admonition to,

"Clean the place up then start to hoe the five acre field."

I swear that if he had been any angrier smoke would have been pouring out of his ears. Retrieving the offensive letter I began to read. It was addressed to me, Clem Branson. You are instructed to report to the military recruiting office located in the federal building at two p.m. on the tenth of this month. I checked the date on the calendar the bean co-op gave us every Christmas. It was already the third, so I had to go there in a week's time. Being unsure what recruiting was, I didn't think too much about it and I couldn't understand why father had gotten so angry. After all, the last time we went to town about the letter in the brown envelope, they just said I could go home after I wrote my name on the paper.

Father remained in an elevated state of anger, with me being the recipient of it for the following week. Mealtimes were an abomination, as father railed on and on with his religious rantings about the government and its inability to follow the teachings of the bible. Why the United States took young innocent God fearing young men and turned them into killing machines and didn't they know that without the young men working on the land, the nation's food supply would dry up. If that happened a biblical plague would descend upon the land just as it had been prophesied. Soldiers of Satan would take over the running of the White House and Congress. Fire and pestilence would consume the people of the earth and the Devils work would be done.

I think my father really believed the claptrap he preached at me non-stop. I didn't, but having said that, I was definitely affected by part of it. As I look back now at father's ranting I believe it was an attempt to brainwash me into sharing his views. But I feel he was the architect of his own failure. Had he treated me with some simple dignity he may have been believable, that is not to say I disbelieved all of it. Constant prayer and regular churchgoing certainly had its effect, I was, and still am a moderately devout Christian.

On the morning of the tenth, father told me I would be going alone and since I needed to go to town anyway, I might as well make myself useful and deliver a load of beans to the elevator. Loaded and tarped, I set off for town. In my mind I transformed the old International five-ton into one of the gleaming eighteen-wheelers I saw burning up the highway miles. I daydreamed of crossing America from coast to coast, all the way to the bean co-op elevator where reality checked in once more. In my shirt pocket the manila envelope served as a constant reminder of my main reason for being in town.

I reported to the recruiting office at the appointed time to find several other young fellows waiting. They took one look at me in my outlandish farm outfit and began to giggle among themselves. Any chance for a sense of camaraderie evaporated. I was different. I knew it already, but it hurt my sense of human dignity to have it thrust upon me this way. I went to sit down away from the other fellows to wait to be called.

A door opened. A soldier stepped into the room His tunic and pants were pressed in razor sharp creases. His boots gleamed jet black with a shine that reflected the light from the glass door and his shirt, tan colored and ironed to a sharp crispness neatly enclosed the tan tie under the collar. Brightly embroidered badges complemented his shoulders; a nametag and medal bar adorned his chest. The soldier wore no hat and his hair cropped short suggested a man of great pride in his appearance.

I had never in my life seen anyone look so smart and I wondered if this was one of the soldiers of Satan that my father had been whining about. From a clipboard he read off a list of names just like Mrs. Bartoski used to do at school.

"Follow me," he said in a commanding voice. He led us into a room with hooks around the wall. "Strip off for your medical exam. Then come into the medical room through this door," he said pointing at the double swinging doors. I felt very uncomfortable. The other young men took of all of their clothing and hung them on the hooks. Father had always insisted nudity to be decadent and sinful, he deemed displaying the human body to others to be the work of degenerates and Satan worshippers. I held back, keeping on my oversize overalls but I did take off my boots and shirt and followed the other naked and seemingly unashamed young men into the examining room.

I must have looked funny to them for they started laughing and pointing at me. A military doctor wearing a white coat over his uniform stepped into the room and stopped in his tracks upon seeing me. Maybe he thought I looked like a circus clown. He stepped right up and stopped within inches of my face.

"Do you have a hearing problem boy?" he bellowed,

"No I don't think so," I replied in innocence of his implied question.

"Then are you a comedian?" Not really sure if a comedian was a person from another county I replied,

"I don't think so." The other young men began to laugh again and I began to feel even more embarrassed.

"What's your name?" the white-coated man asked me.

"Clem,"

"Clem who?" Are you playing games with me boy?"

"It's Clem Branson." I began to sweat. I knew the man was making sport of me and I didn't understand why.

"When you are instructed to strip, you are expected to strip Branson. Get rid of those ridiculous overalls." I slipped the straps off my shoulders and the loose garment fell around my ankles. My envelope of documents flew out of the chest pocket and slid across the floor, I attempted to stop it tripping over my overalls and landing on the floor face down. The group of naked men bent over slapped their knees and burst into gales of laughter. I had never felt more vulnerable in my entire life. I, the unwilling center of attention, struggled to my feet clutching the envelope. I saw in the face of the doctor fellow the same look of disgust and derision I had seen in my father's so many times before.

"Settle down and stand in a straight line," the doctor ordered us. One at a time he conducted his examination of our bodies, leaving me until last. He wrote some things on my papers and said I could get dressed and sit and wait for my recruiting officer's interview. As I pulled on my overalls I noticed the black line of mud and bean dust around my lower legs. The other young men watched me get dressed and when I placed my stained straw hat upon my head; they again burst into gales of uncontrolled merriment. I sat on the plain wood bench under the clothing hooks feeling utterly alone knowing I did not fit in with general society. Finally they called me in for my interview.

"Why does the army want to talk to me? Why have you brought me here? Back at our farm we have a bean crop to harvest in the near future," I asked the uniformed soldier. "My father says I am needed at home to work the farm."

"There is a war going on in Korea. Uncle Sam needs all the able bodied young men he can get."

"Why is your Uncle having a war? Is he mad at someone?" He looked at me very strangely, kind of like he didn't understand my question.

"Uncle Sam is a euphemism for the United States son. Are you not aware there is a military conflict going on in Korea?"

"No. What is Korea?"

"Do you not listen to the radio at your home Branson?"

"No Sir. My father won't have one on the farm he says it is an instrument of the devil."

"How much schooling have you had Branson?"

"I used to go to Mrs. Bartoski's house for learning, but father stopped me from going when I was still small. He said I had to help on the farm after we buried my mother in the churchyard."

"Clem your medical exam shows you are a strong healthy young man and you will be drafted into the army. We will teach you a whole new series of skills.

34

Tell me? What kind of work would you like to do while you are in the army Clem?" I thought for a long time before I answered him. I thought about the pleasure I got from driving the bean truck and how I daydreamed it might be a big shiny Freightliner or Mack. Gage County to this Korea place and back again. Without any further hesitation I replied,

"Be a truck driver."

"Do you know how to cook, Clem?"

"Yes. I have been cooking for father and I since mother died."

"I think you would fit well in the catering corps, Clem. Yes. I am going to put you down for catering. You will be having what we call basic training for the first couple of months and then your officers will make a final decision on your deployment. Welcome to the United States Army, Clem Branson." He held his hand out to me and I thought he wanted to give me something, but he just wanted to shake it. You can go home now Clem. Get your business in order you should hear from us in a week to ten days, we will send you your travel documents and instructions on where you are to report." As I turned to leave I detected him stifle a laugh as he saw me walk away in my ridiculous clothes.

On the way back to the farm I wondered how I would tell father I was going to be a truck driver in the army and if he would be pleased for me. Or might he be angry with the army for taking his farm worker away so close to bean harvesting. In my heart I knew the answer remembering I never saw my father smile.

My father certainly didn't break his unenviable record and smile on this day. He became so angry when

I told him the army wanted me to drive a truck for them, I thought he had gone completely mad. When I told him I would likely be gone in a week's time he lost control and proceeded to hurl the furniture around. Then began the vitriolic tirade of religious ranting, just as suddenly as it had begun, the rampage ended. Father stormed from the kitchen and I picked up the furnishings and put them back where they belonged. I heard the engine of the International five-ton, burst angrily into life and a cloud of Gage County dust rose skywards following the vehicle as it sped from the yard.

I finished tidying up the mess in the kitchen then took my hoe and began to scarify the soil in the vegetable garden. Working my hoe deftly between the plants my mind uncluttered with other things, I wondered if father would take care of the garden as mother and I always had. He had never put any effort at all into the garden, 'Woman's work.' He would declare. I looked at the tomatoes, they were just coming into maximum production and I wondered if they would rot on the vine. I didn't think he would bother to preserve them in mason jars like mother had shown me how to do. All I knew at this moment was that I would do my duty here on the farm until the day I left. I had almost finished scarifying the entire garden, when looking up I saw the truck approaching.

I fully expected my father to renew his verbal assaults upon me as soon as he had parked, but no sooner than he had, when I observed two figures climbing down from the rear of the bean box and then father dismounted from the cab. He walked toward them and led the pair to the tractor shed. Now I could tell one of the strangers wore a dress. For the life of me I could not understand why father would bring strangers to the farm let alone a woman. My curiosity got the better of me despite the feeling that father would likely begin to yell; I wandered over to where they stood looking into the tractor shed.

Drawing closer, I saw they were black folks. I had seen a few at times in while in town but I had never talked to one. The Gage County farmers called them nigras. And some had another word. I had learned from snatches of conversation that white folks like us generally didn't associate with nigras, although some did work on a few farms within the County.

The nigras turned to look as I approached. My father pointed at me,

"He's Clem." He said, not elaborating on our relationship. The nigra woman smiled at me. It was a wonderful moment. Not since mother died had a lady smiled at me, I returned her smile with a wide grin and my eyes glistened with the joy of the moment. The lady's skin shone like clean silverware reflecting the Gage County sun. Very dark eyes warmed me from each side of a wide but friendly nose bone white teeth glistened from between her ample lips. She wore a sunbonnet tied with ribbon under her chin and a long light colored dress with dust stains at the hem above her ankles and scuffed shoes. I did not know who this lady was or the reason she stood before me. But I did know I liked her. The man with her appeared to be a strong muscular man with his tight black hair beginning to show traces of early gray. He wore overalls like father and I, but his were not too large or long and fit him better. In his hand he held a battered suitcase and he too gave me a wide smile. Not a smile of pretense, but of genuine pleasure to greet me.

"I can find you sufficient lumber to board up the shed front and I can find an old door somewhere around the place. Boy! Go in the house and begin bringing the spare bed out to the shed here." My father said curtly. I had no idea what had occurred since father had left the house after running amok. Not willing to get into an unpleasant altercation with him, I went to the house and began dismantling the spare bed which had lain unused since the day Grandmother walked out. When I returned to the shed with the headboard, father and the man were packing old lumber and plywood in, when I brought out the footboard the black man was starting to build a wall across the old doorway.

I knew it would be pointless to ask my father what is going on; he likely wouldn't answer me anyway. While father brought more wood from behind the bean silo, I asked the lady,

"Why are you here? What is happening?" She answered me in a soft and gentle voice,

"Your father tells us you are going to the army in a few days. He will have no one to help with the harvest and to run his house with you gone and so he hired us. I am to cook, see to the garden and clean the house. My husband, Amos is to work the fields with your father."

"But why are you changing the tractor shed?"

"It is obvious that you are an extremely innocent young man, Clem. Black folks don't live in the same house as whites. Amos and I will sleep in the tractor shed and take our meals out on the kitchen porch."

"But why?"

"We will get into that at another time Clem. It's a centuries old story."

I brought the balance of the bed pieces out and the woman helped me put it together at the back wall.

"What do folks call you?" I asked between the noise of the hammering and sawing.

"My mother named me, Elizabeth. But everyone calls me, Liza."

"Why do folks call you nigras? That is not your surname is it?

"No Clem. The word is Negroes. Saying nigras is just poor local speech, just as people say overhauls instead of overalls. Our surname is, Washington."

Mrs. Washington went about fixing up the tractor shed as a home for her and Amos and I went to finish cultivating the garden vowing I would never use the word nigra again.

When I had completed the garden work I went about my other regular evening chores then went to the house to begin preparing the evening meal. To my surprise Liza had already begun, but instead of food preparations for two, she busily made sufficient for four.

"Leave it to me Clem," she said when I moved to help. "I'm used to cooking for more than two." I thought I would take the opportunity to ask Liza what she meant by saying it's a century old story.

"What do you know about American history Clem?"

"I know that when the pilgrims came they ate turkeys. Mrs. Bartoski told us that at school but we don't have turkeys in Gage County."

"Is that all you know Clem?"

"Just about, I didn't go to school for very long, I had to leave to help my father on the farm."

"Has no one told you about slavery and the almost non acceptance of the slaves when finally they were freed?"

"Don't think so Liza. If they did I don't remember. Mostly I learn about the bible from my father's readings and I learned how to grow good quality beans, take care of the house and cooking. I know how to preserve our vegetables, my mother showed me before we buried her in the churchyard. I like to whittle too I'm pretty good at it." It felt so good to have someone to talk to and even better to have someone listen and seem interested.

"Well Clem. I won't go into it too deeply but just to say that most white folks look down upon blacks. We are not deemed to be as valuable human beings as whites. Some of it may be religion based, some perhaps because they would like to see us as slaves again. A goodly number of whites feel radically superior to blacks and I suppose there are other reasons too like social stigma. That's when whites will not eat alongside blacks, share a source of drinking water, or sleep under the same roof as blacks in case they are thought badly of by other whites and that, Clem is why, Amos and I will be living in your tractor shed and eating our meals on the kitchen porch."

I sat down by the stove watching the pots boil and considering what Liza had told me. I asked myself is my father one of these people with this stigma thing she mentioned. It seemed very confusing. Father often in his prayers and bible reading spoke of love thy neighbor as thyself. Forcing the Washington's to live in the tractor shed was a direct contradiction of his and the bible's words. Not only that, I began to think his treatment of me didn't ring true to those words either.

"Would you mind going to tell the men the meal is ready, Clem?" I noticed she had set the table for two and set two more plates out on the wide porch railing. I called father and Amos and went back to the house. When father and I were seated, I remarked that I didn't think we should make the Washington's eat outside. Without a second's hesitation he stood and punched me with all his might on my left cheek.

"You had better learn your place in this world boy. The lion shall not sleep with the lamb." I no longer cried when father assaulted me. I had grown too old to allow him to see how he hurt me. But he did hurt me. Inside I felt shame and anger both at him and his edicts. I left the table with my meal uneaten and went to sit and contemplate behind the bean silos. I suppose out of habit I took my whittling knife from my pocket and began working on a piece of scrap wood. I could have worked faster and better had I gone to the house for my carving set, but I resolved I would not and have to pass my father in the kitchen. In an hour or so I turned the scrap of wood into a dove with outspread wings and took and gave it to Liza.

"Why thank you Clem. Did you make this yourself?"

"Yes. I just made it since supper."

"It is beautiful Clem. You are a talented young man. I shall put it in my new home and look at it often. Did you know the dove represents peace and harmony?"

"No," I replied. I felt so good in my heart that Liza liked the carving. Not since mother died had anyone expressed any interest in them. Most of what I had already carved, my father had burned in the stove. I began to blush with pride at Liza's words, even more so when she took it to Amos. He turned it over and over in his big hands.

"You should be proud of this young man, it is very good. Sit with us a while and talk."

"How did my father find you? How did he know you would come out to work at the Branson bean farm?"

"He went to the church. The pastor has been kindly giving us food and shelter and when your father came to ask about some help on the farm, he introduced us. We were grateful for the offer of work and a place to stay."

"It is not much of a place to live in Amos. I am ashamed that father is making you stay in the tractor shed and not in the house."

"Well young fellow. Just think about it for a minute. Will Liza and I not be better off in here than in the house listening to your father preaching all the time." I did think about it and realized that Amos was no fool, he had father well and truly figured out already. I had become so starved for conversation that I might have overstayed my welcome that first night the Washington's came to live at the farm. I remember it had become quite late when I left them to go to father's prayer session and my bed in the house.

What an amazing change had taken place overnight on the Branson bean farm. Liza busied herself making breakfast when I arose. Lighting the stove and making the oatmeal had always been my job until today. Outside, Amos was tidying up the farmyard; I cannot recall it had ever been done before. After breakfast Amos followed me around as I did my regular chores, learning how father would have it done after I had gone to the army truck-driving place. Then he I and father worked the bean rows until Liza called us for lunch. Father sat at the table with his bible open so I went out to join the Washington's on the porch.

In the space of twenty-four hours something amazing had happened. I no longer saw, Amos and Liza as black people. I saw them only as people, but as kind gentle caring people no longer distinguishable by color. In them, I saw something that had been missing from my life thus far. I spent every moment of my spare time in their company.

Another manila envelope arrived in the mailbox. Father handed it to me unopened without a single word. I wondered if he had washed his hands of me now that the Washington's were here. Inside the envelope were a list of instructions on how to get to Camp Moresby and a railroad voucher. The train I had to ride, left three days from now. I told my father I had to leave on Thursday and he just shrugged, saying nothing. I told the Washington's when I would be leaving and they both wished me luck.

"Do you know what to expect in the army, Clem?" Liza asked me the night before my departure. I replied,

"Yes they are going to give me a truck to drive."

"Didn't you say you were going to the catering corps, Clem?"

"Then don't be surprised if there is no truck, Clem. The army has a way of changing expectations."

"How do you mean Liza?"

"Amos and I had twin boys once, Clem. It was 1943 and they were drafted together. The army said they would not be separated or sent to an active war zone but they sent them to Europe and they are both buried somewhere over there." I saw a tear come to Liza's dark eyes and slide down her shiny cheek and I found I had nothing I could say. When it came time for me to leave them to spend my last night in the Branson farmhouse, Liza hugged me and whispered,

"Take good care of yourself, Clem Branson." I had never been hugged since mother hugged me before she died. With warm loving arms holding me the sudden thought of mother and the farewell, Liza and, Amos were giving me brought tears to my own eyes. I felt no shame at these tears and encircled in Liza's arms I wept the tears of a lost child finding a mother.

Since I had never owned or needed a suitcase, I left the Branson farmhouse with a clean hand-me-down shirt and my beloved carving kit wrapped in my other pair of overalls. Father drove the bean truck in his usual fashion with eyes front never seeing the beauty of the landscape and his mouth firmly closed. I wondered how our parting would go, would father finally show some emotion at my leaving or be his cold miserable self. On the silent ride to the train station I felt a sense of fear and foreboding.

Today I stepped albeit unwillingly, into a world of the unknown. I had never been on a train before nor had I ever ventured outside of Gage County, my entire existence had taken place on the Branson bean farm. It would be a falsehood to say I had been happy there, I hadn't, at least not since mother died. But the farm had always been my secure place despite father's frequent bursts of religious rhetoric and violence. As the old International bounced and clattered along I began to think of Liza and Amos. I had known them but a week, but in that fleeting week they had carved a permanent place in my heart. Liza had shown me more love and understanding in those few days than I had known my whole life. Instinctively I knew the love should have come from my family but it hadn't and now I leaped into a new and frightening phase of my life with no emotional backup to gird my loins.

We neared the edge of town. Not even a grunt had passed fathers lips and I felt sure now there would be no emotional farewell. Frankly had there been, I should not have known how to handle it. A kind or loving word from father would be completely foreign to both of us. He stopped the truck outside the train depot, stared straight ahead and when I alighted he let out the clutch, a puff of blue smoke enveloped me and he was gone. No farewell. No good luck son. No may God take care of you. Then I remembered once again that in my entire life, I never saw my father smile.

CHAPTER THREE.

The blue cloud of acrid smelling smoke from the truck engine, drifted away from me slowly rising into the crisp morning air. I watched the brake lights go on as the truck slowed for the corner then it disappeared from view. I stood outside the railroad station feeling deserted and very much alone, aware that this was a defining moment in my life. I had a genuine feeling that father had just simply abandoned me to a fate unknown. He had discarded his only son as if I were a nameless hitchhiker without a single word of goodbye. I wondered if he had considered that he might never set eyes on me again. Did he feel anything about dropping me off here as if I were no better than a load of his beans or the hog we slaughtered every year? I cannot describe to you the terrible feeling of having no value as a person, to feel unloved and utterly alone and to wish that God would take me, here right now. The excitement I had felt earlier this week about the new and unknown life I faced in the army, died in my breast amid the blue smoke cloud of my father's departure.

I knew I had to get a grip of myself. God would not take me but the army would and I would take the army. I stood, poised to embrace my new life wearing shabby boots worn without socks, patched and worn overalls showing bare leg between my boot tops and my knees. A shirt faded and much too small for the body it encompassed and my stained and shabby straw hat. Gripping my bundle I walked into the small whistle-stop station.

"She's running a little late this morning son, there will be a thirty minute wait," the station man told me after looking at me oddly and examining my ticket. "Going to fight for our country are you son?"

"No. I'm going to drive a truck for the army. How long will it take to get to this Camp Moresby place?" I asked.

"If there are no further delays, you should arrive about three pm tomorrow afternoon."

"Then it must be a long way how far is it?"

"It's close to the west coast. I don't recall the exact mileage." Since I had been too nervous to eat Liza's breakfast, I figured by tomorrow afternoon I would be really hungry.

"Is there food on the train?" I asked.

"Yes of course there is son you can get your meals in the dining car." Mild panic hit me. Father had never given me money for working for him; I didn't mind that for I thought it was my Christian duty. It had never occurred to me I would need money on the journey, everything I had ever bought in the past got charged to our account at the bean co-op General Store. More ill feelings about my father came to me, adding to the ones I already harbored in my heart. I could not help but wonder if he had sent me out into an unfamiliar world penniless on purpose. But why would he do that? He must have known I would need some traveling money; I remembered father reading aloud the parable of the prodigal son from the bible, at this moment it seemed meaningless.

I sat on a bench awaiting the train. A loud whistle in the distance announced its approach; the clanging bell and hissing steam confirmed the train's arrival. The station man had told me I would be riding in the last car and so I climbed the two steps and found an unoccupied seat and placed my bundle on it and sat in a high backed soft chair the softest I had ever been in. After a few minutes the train began to move, taking me away from Gage County and all I had ever known. Fields with crops I was not familiar with flashed by the windows, streams and lakes small towns and large cities, forestland and wide rivers. I saw them all until the sun set and now dim lights appeared to be rushing by.

I had developed a mighty thirst and so I went to see if I could find some drinking water. A man directed me to a lavatory in the rear of the railcar. Not only did I find drinking water I found a place where I could go to have a pee. The receptacle did not resemble anything I had ever seen before. Since I hadn't been since I left the farm, I felt highly relieved. Also I could wash my hands and face in the smallest dishwashing sink I had ever seen. I had much to see and learn in this new and unusual world I had been thrust into. I filled my stomach with water using the little paper cup and I remember thinking how the thing could never hold hot coffee.

I returned to my seat and prepared to spend the night in a sitting position. Some one tapped on my shoulder. I looked up and a lady wearing a flowered hat spoke in my ear. It surprised me. I'm not a good judge of ages, but she appeared to be about forty-five to fifty years old and had a chubby cheeked motherly kind of face and her eyes had a kindly expression. As the lady stepped alongside me I saw she wore a frilly white blouse buttoned to the neck and a sort of jacket in a dark color. Her skirt had pleats from her waist to the hemline and on her legs wore stocking in a light tan color and I saw she had on fancy shoes, not the work boots I was used to seeing folks wear.

"I haven't seen you go to the dining car or eat anything out of your bundle young man." Her words surprised me. Who was she, why did she care if I had not eaten?

"I have no money Ma'am," I answered truthfully.

"Where are you going to, will you be arriving at home soon?"

"I'm going to Camp Moresby Ma'am. I am going to the army."

"My goodness, you won't get there until tomorrow afternoon. Have you had anything at all to eat today?"

"No Ma'am."

"I have a couple of apples and a banana in my bag will you accept them?"

"Yes Ma'am I would, for I am fair famished. Thank you for your kindness."

"You are welcome young man." The lady gave me the fruit and I devoured them. "Do you mind if I sit with you for a while," she asked me. Busy eating, I shook my head. "Why have you no money?" she inquired. I told her father hadn't given me any. "It seems odd that the military would not give you a travel allowance. Let me see your ticket." I removed it from my overalls breast pocket and handed it to her. She studied on in for a moment then said, "This ticket contains meal vouchers. Did no one explain it to you?"

"No Ma'am what does it mean?"

"It means you can go to the dining car for your meals. The army has paid for them, but the dining car has closed for the day. However you will be able to go for breakfast in the morning and have a proper meal." She asked me where I had come from, and about the life I had led until today. Like Liza, she was easy to talk to and we did talk, right into the middle of the night. It seemed odd; within the space of seven days I had enjoyed more conversation than I had in most of my existence. Mrs. Wilson told me about her life growing up with a large number of siblings and how wonderful her young life had been with games and fun and trips in the car with her family. How her parents loved each other and lavished the love on their children. She told of how during the war she had worked in a big factory in the state of Michigan making airplane parts for the war effort. I learned how she had met her future husband and how they were parted by his service in the navy. She told me sadly how he had contracted cancer and passed away just months earlier. Mrs. Wilson said she planned to visit her favorite sister in Los Angeles to recover emotionally from her grief. When Mrs. Wilson went back to her seat I curled up to try and sleep. The rocking and noise of the train made it difficult and in a state between sleep and troubled wakefulness I could not help but compare her young life against mine and the scales were not tipped in my favor.

I must have slept eventually, for when I opened my eyes daylight streamed through my window. Outside, the landscape was unlike anything I had ever seen before. We were passing through parched desert like terrain, stunted and dead trees, brown shrubs and bare rocks littered the land. My first thought, beans would never grow here. My stomach growled and my throat felt parched. Mrs. Wilson must have seen me stirring and came to my seat,

"Go and wash your face Clem and then you can come with me to the dining car for breakfast." I felt very grateful she had asked me. I had never eaten in a public place before and I felt embarrassed because I did not know what to expect, or how to conduct myself. I suspect that Mrs. Wilson understood how I would feel, since in our long conversation I had told her how I had virtually no life experiences except bean farming and that I had eaten in the same chair and at the same table without exception since I had been weaned.

She led the way through the train to the dining car. I saw the many faces of the other passengers as they looked up and saw me follow Mrs. Wilson. I look back now on that morning and the smirks and looks of disparagement and realize that they probably thought that I was her mentally challenged child dressed in the most appalling apparel with my hair having the appearance of having been dragged through the bushes backwards. In retrospect Mrs. Wilson had a great deal of compassion. She could like many others have ignored completely, the country bumpkin on his first train ride. She asked me what I would like to eat and ordered it. I wolfed down my food ravenously, slurped my coffee and wiped my mouth on my shirtsleeve since I did not understand the purpose of the table napkin before me. Sniggers could be heard from surrounding tables as the diners watched me in amusement and I presume disgust, at my lack of social skills. Mrs. Wilson gave them icy stares but continued to give me motherly smiles.

When we returned to our seats in the rear car, she again sat with me.

"Clem," she said. "From what have told me, you are stepping into a world you have no experience in. There will be some who will take you to task for it, others will mock you and try to bring you down. Possibly others will use violence upon your person and your first few weeks in the military could be filled with ridicule and ill treatment. I am telling you this, Clem not because I wish to frighten you, but rather so that you can be prepared. You can be strong and resilient or you can be weak and let them destroy your pride and self-worth. You are a fine young man, Clem Branson. Sadly it appears your own family has done you a great dis-service and it will take time for you to learn the ways of the real world."

Mrs. Wilson left me and returned to her seat. I reflected upon her words. She had spoken the truth. Yes. My father had let me down in the most appalling way and yet I could not bring myself to hate him. Right now I despised father, but I did not hate him.

At noon she took me to lunch with her in the dining car. She whispered,

"Clem, watch and imitate how I use my cutlery and napkin. Let's show the people around us you know how." I did as she suggested and the process of my learning table manners began.

We talked the afternoon away, and then the conductor stepped into the railcar and announced the next stop would be Camp Moresby. Mrs. Wilson's enjoyable company and the quiet conversations with her ended abruptly and the fear of the unknown re-entered my breast.

I clutched my bundle tightly and stepped from the train. Wondering which way I had to go to find the army camp and how far I would have to walk to get there I thought I should ask someone. A dozen or so young men about my age stood by the train looking just as bewildered as I. A smartly dressed soldier walked up to us carrying a clipboard like the one the weigh master at the bean co-op had.

"When I call your name answer loudly then come and stand behind me." He almost shouted the words as if he were angry with us. He called out names and those called went and stood behind him.

"Clement Branson!" I heard my name and began to walk to get behind him. He glanced at me then stopped calling out the rest of the names. He stepped up to me, looked me up and down with a sneer rapidly forming on his face.

"Well. Doggone if we don't have a hayseed hillbilly with us. What have you got in the bundle, hillbilly, Chitlins and possum gizzards?"

"No. Just my clean overalls and shirt and my carving kit."

"So you intend to wear overalls in the United States Army do you, hillbilly?"

"It depends if I have dirty work to do."

"Hillbilly, I can guarantee that you will. How dare you come to camp looking like a circus clown? You are an idiot, hillbilly. Get behind me." He called out the rest of the names and led us to a truck with a canvas cover over the bed. I wondered if the truck might be the one they were going to give me to drive.

"Is this my truck?" I asked in all innocence. The soldier exploded in anger. If you are attempting to try my patience, hillbilly you are doing a great job. The other young men were doubled up with laughter and it seemed to make the soldier livid. His face turned beet red and the veins on his neck stood out throbbing like the hose on our farm water pump.

"In the truck!" he shrieked at us and we scrambled up the tailboard and sat on board seats down each side. One man spoke,

"You have managed to get him truly pissed off at us now, hillbilly, thanks a whole bunch." I didn't really understand the statement since I had just asked a simple question. I had not intended it to be rude or to make the soldier angry. The truck began moving with a mighty jerk sending us all flying down the long seats. I believe I said the driver needed a few lessons in letting out a clutch. In retrospect, I think I should have kept my mouth shut, for the men began a verbal attack calling me scarecrow, circus clown and a hillbilly know-it-all. What happened next didn't endear me to them either. The truck stopped about a mile from the camp gates and the soldier ordered us out.

"Every damn one of you morons start running! Any slackers will rue the day your mother allowed you to breathe!" We had to run as fast as we could with the

truck following and the soldier yelling profanities at us through the open windshield. I didn't mind the running, I was used to strenuous activity, but my heels and ankles hurt from having no socks in my boots.

From the moment I entered the camp gates, until the time I became inconspicuous dressed in my army uniform, I was a laughing stock dressed in my farm overalls. It seems the word of my hillbilly appearance traveled throughout the camp and I collected a great deal of names, none of which was Clem Branson. I felt extreme gratitude to Mrs. Wilson from the train for her warning of what I might expect for it stood me in good stead. I refused to be upset at the name-calling, accepting it instead as humor. After the training in emotional restraint I had received at my father's hand it really wasn't very difficult.

I discovered why they called it boot camp. We new recruits were issued brand new boots. I had never owned a pair that fit me properly and felt so proud especially since they gave me socks too. They gave me a uniform and smart shirts as well as a complete set of work clothes. I had never owned so many clothes and I felt humbled and grateful. We were shown how to take care of our clothing and always have it smart looking. We were told our boots had to be polished until the drill sergeant could see his reflection in them. Many of the men grumbled and complained but I felt so proud to have new footwear I worked for hours in a labor of love to have the shiniest boots in the camp.

The drill sergeant worked us hard. It did not distress me in the least, being fit and strong from constant work on the farm. My initial appearance at boot camp set the tone for the rest of my time there. The drill sergeant always referred to me as hillbilly he would scream it right into my face as I stood to attention, I knew it was his aim to break me down but I always thought of Mrs. Wilson's words and allowed his insults to slide off me like dry beans down the elevator chute. Some of my fellow recruits were not quite as lucky as I, at night in the barracks I could often hear muffled sobs from young men whose hearts, minds, and spirits were broken by the regime of constant work and verbal assaults.

Throughout the roughest times I told myself it would all end soon when I had learned how to march, shoot a gun straight, and to take good care of my equipment. I always kept it front in my mind that they would soon give me a truck to drive like the man in the recruiting office had said. I must admit during my six week's at boot camp I rarely thought about my father and the farm, every day being chock full of things to do and new things to learn. To the army's credit, my fellow recruits and I were changed men at the end of six weeks. We were all stronger fitter and much more knowledgeable on a variety of subjects. I felt especially proud of how I looked in the mirror dressed in my uniform. No longer a visible misfit, I had shaken off the feel and look of the country bumpkin who ran through the camp gates six weeks ago.

"You sorry bunch of humanity will be going on a graduation parade tomorrow. My future as a drill sergeant rests on how you perform in front of the brass. Screw it up and I will have you for the next six weeks, you will think the last six were like being in kindergarten." The drill sergeant stood in front of each of us individually and yelled directly into our faces, "I have tried to make a man out of you soldier. You may face rough times ahead. If you do, think of me as being right behind you and you will find the strength to do what you have to do."

The drill sergeant led us into the parade. We marched with heads held high and shoulders back, our boots and uniforms spotless and our rifles gleaming and ready for action. I guess we did all right, for after parade we were paid and given ten days leave. For the first time in my life I had cash money in my pants pocket. Most of the new soldiers were eager to go home to their parents for the ten days. I had no inclination to return to the farm and have my newfound pride crushed under my father's foot, nor had I had any intention of returning to be unpaid farm labor.

Ralph Watson from New York, Frank Pittello from Indiana and Hank Matson from Chicago, were like myself from unhappy or broken homes and had no wish to waste our furlough time going back. When I told them that in my entire life I had never seen my father smile, they convinced me I should accompany them for what they termed a wild time in the city. Frankly I didn't need much convincing, working the bean farm or a wild time in the city it was a pretty easy choice for me to make.

Never in my life had I consumed alcohol or beer. Such things by my father at the Branson farm were considered evil potions fit only for the devil and his cohorts. He claimed even the communion wine in some religious denominations were proof of the devils infiltration. Their congregations will burn in hell for all eternity while we the righteous will look down upon them in pity. Obviously the sermons from his pulpit at the kitchen stove had some effect upon me, how could it have been otherwise? So it was with some trepidation I drank my first glass of beer with my three military friends. If it were their intention to get me stinking drunk on our first night away from the confines of the camp they succeeded magnificently. After the first five beers I have no recollection of what happened afterwards. I woke up in a dingy hotel room with my stomach urgently prompting me to puke and puke I did. Once my body had been purged of the concoction of unremembered Chinese food and festering beer, my friends tried to convince me that I had a great time last night. Hank Matson asked,

"Have you ever been laid, Clem?"

During the last six weeks in the camp surrounded by other young men among the myriad of things I had learned, was that getting laid meant having been with a woman and committed fornication with her. Such subjects were of course taboo at the Branson farm and therefore I had basically no knowledge of such things and I most certainly was not guilty of the sin. I had of course listened with great interest to my comrades and the tales of their conquests but I had listened in silence. But now the question had been hurled at my feet and I had to respond truthfully.

"No." I answered shyly. "I know nothing about such things except for what I have heard you guys saying in camp." All three of my companions began laughing.

"Clem, my country bumpkin buddy, it's time you discovered the charms of the fairer sex. Today we your friends will get you laid for the very first time." Frank Pittello said,

"Surely you are kidding us Clem. You mean you have

never dipped your wick?" I knew what he meant and I began to feel really embarrassed and sweat poured from my brow. I knew I was completely and utterly ignorant of the facts of life, other than our bean flowers required the honeybees to mix the pollen to make beans happen. I had however become used to male nudity in the camp and I had overcome my extreme shyness, but the thought of using or displaying my male parts with a woman terrified me, even the thought of such behaviour made me sweat profusely.

"Some other time guys," I protested, "I really don't feel very well after drinking all that beer and barfing."

"What you need, Clem Branson is a hair of the dog that bit you."

"I don't remember being bitten. Was it last night?"

"Goofball! When you get a hangover from beer you drink a little more and the feeling goes away then you feel good again," Ralph Watson informed me the meaning of the dog bite words while handing over an open can of Budweiser. I drank Ralph's patent medicine in two gulps and then we went in search of a place to have breakfast.

I think it was the bacon, eggs, hash browns and toast with a half gallon of black coffee making me feel better not Ralph's professed cure. After we had all eaten we drifted round the streets until the guys discovered a pool hall. Here I found myself in another of my father's stated dens of sin. I wondered how he would react if he had any inkling how far down the path to Hell I had strayed within the space of twenty-four hours. But I reasoned, judging by his past general attitude towards me, he really wouldn't care and indeed why should I, for had I not lived most of my life in a Hell of his making?

My friends were very patient with me, they tried to teach me how to play pool unfortunately I could not get the hang of hitting the little white ball with the end of the stick and Hank, my partner lost every game. After a couple of hours it was agreed we go get some more beer. We sat until the evening shadows began to fall across the tavern window. I had been carefully avoiding drinking too much; I had no appetite for a repeat of last night's performance.

Hank Matson stood up and announced,

"It is time to bring our good friend, Clem into the twentieth century." I was not totally sure what Hank meant, but I had a feeling he referred to having me go with a woman for fornication. I began to sweat again.

"Maybe tomorrow," I protested.

"Bullshit Clem, we are going to get you laid today. Let's go boys." My friends escorted me out of the tavern and into a taxi. Hank spoke softly to the driver who proceeded to take us into a rather seedy area of the city. The cab stopped on a street where a number of girls leaned against the building walls. Frank and Ralph left us to talk to two girls down the block, while Hank pulled me along to a girl who looked very nice to me. She wore her hair tied in the back with a big red bow, her skirt seemed very short and I wondered if she would be warm enough in it. Her blouse was cut so low I was surprised she didn't catch a chest cold for it revealed a good portion of her breasts just like in the magazines the guys had back in the barracks. She had on the highest heeled shoes I have ever seen and I remember thinking she would be much more comfortable walking with a pair of good work boots.

Hank spoke to her while I hung back. I was very much afraid I would soon have to face up to my fears of this proposed encounter. Hank grabbed my arm and we began following the girl to a crummy looking hotel. Hank passed some money to the character behind the wicket in the narrow lobby and then we followed the girl upstairs where she opened a door and went inside.

Closing the door behind us Hank said to the girl,

"It's his first time. Show him the ropes, I will be watching." The girl stripped off her clothing and lay on the bed. I stared in wonder at her body. Sweat oozed from every pore in my body. My breathing came in short heavy pants. Nothing in my life had prepared me for this moment and I felt intense discomfort and fear.

"Get your gear off Clem. She's waiting for it." Hank said. I stripped and lay on the bed with her. I knew my body was supposed to prepare me to get laid, but nothing happened. The girl tried to help me but still nothing happened. After a few moments, I guess Hank became impatient with me.

"Don't tell me you are a Goddamn queer, Clem. Get out of the way, I paid the broad and if you don't want it, I do!" I felt awful. I had let Hank down and I felt devastated that I could not achieve the necessary erection to get laid. Hank stripped and lay atop the girl and proceeded to do it. My fear of the girl being hurt by the act of penetration, left when I clearly saw it didn't. The vision of Hank in obvious enjoyment with the girl caused me to cast aside my fear and I was more than ready when he rolled off her. I took my turn and discovered for the first time the joy, the exquisite feeling and wonder of getting laid. I knew the experience had ended when an intense feeling consumed me leaving me gasping for air. This was the moment the boys in the barrack room all talked about. Despite the magnificence of the experience, I had a distinct feeling something was missing. It's hard to explain, sort of like I had used the girl for my own pleasure and she had accommodated me. But I felt no affection or closeness from her and I felt none for her. Deep down I sensed I had violated her.

Hank threw some bills on the bed and then he and I dressed and went back out to the street.

"Jeez Clem! I never thought I would ever have to show a guy how to get laid, I thought you were a Goddamn fairy at first."

"I was scared, Hank. I didn't want to hurt her."

"From what I've seen Clem, you sure don't have enough to do that."

We rejoined Frank and Ralph and they too had got laid. We went together to drink more beer then went back to our hotel to sleep. I lay awake staring at the shadows creeping across the drapes from the traffic in the street below. I could not get the encounter with the girl out of my mind. Getting laid was beautiful and I wanted more, lots more. However the feelings of guilt I had experienced earlier nagged at me. I wondered if my feelings were of concern for the girl or the religious teachings of my father regarding fornication impeding my own free thoughts.

It had bothered me somewhat when Hank told the others how I had failed to rise to the occasion until he showed me how to do it. They laughed, but soon the incident had been forgotten. For the next three days we drank beer and got laid as often as we could afford, then utterly broke we walked back to camp and spent the rest of our furlough in the barracks. With my money gone and time on my hands, I began to think of my father and how the bean crop harvesting had been. I thought too of Eliza and Amos and I wondered if my father was treating them properly and if he preached his unending fire and brimstone to them. It occurred to me I should write to him to let him know how his son had become a smart soldier and that I was well, but I thought better of it, when I remembered because never having seen my father smile, he would likely not welcome such a letter from the son he seemed to despise.

The rest of our troop returned to barracks at the end of the ten-day furlough. We were ordered to an assignment parade where we would be told our destination and allotted military jobs. I hoped Frank, Ralph, and Hank and I would be shipped out together we had become good friends having the kinship of a background of dysfunctional families. Sadly the military brass saw fit to split us up and after the day of departure I never saw Hank or Ralph ever again. We had been told that most of us would be going overseas to fight in Korea. I have often wondered in the intervening years if my friends had been killed and their bodied buried there. Of course my own dream of driving a large truck across America to Korea had been dashed, when I had been informed Korea was a land far across the Pacific Ocean.

Frank Pittello and I traveled together to a camp near the ocean in California. Upon reporting for duty I felt extreme disappointment, we were to be split up. Frank went to an infantry division, while I had to report to the camp catering corps as a catering trainee. Deep down

I hoped that they would give me a truck driver's job, but I had severe misgivings which turned out to be well founded. I reported to the commanding officer of the catering corps with every crease in my uniform and shirt ironed to perfection and my boots shining like the California sun.

He took my papers, looked at them and said brusquely,

"Report to the head chef." I found him in the rear of the huge mess tent wearing his fatigues, a tall white chefs hat and apron, with a half smoked unlit stogie hanging from his surly lips. He glanced at the paper I had handed him, and then he spoke with a snarl that sounded in tone incredibly like my fathers voice,

"Get into your fatigues soldier I have got just the job for you." I went to my assigned barrack, changed clothes then re-reported to the chef.

"I'm Sergeant Daly, Branson. I don't take crap from anybody nor do I suffer fools. You will be on dishwashing duty until I decide you are fit to do anything different. Your induction documents state you are used to kitchen work. That's good, Branson, because it is what you will get lots of here." I felt anger rising in my breast towards my father. I realized instantly the way I had been dressed when I went to enlist, had a direct bearing on what was now happening to me. I had obviously been perceived as mentally incapable of anything but dishwashing. Did my father know how things would go for his son? Had he sent me there dressed that way purposely? I could not help but wonder if my father hated me as much as he professed to hate the Devil. My father's odious treatment of me now had taken away my dream of being a driver. I felt it was not an unreasonable dream and it was something I could do equally as well as washing enormous piles of dishes.

Sergeant Daly led me to a massive stainless steel sink unit, piled high at one end with large rectangular cooking utensils, plates, cups and an assortment of dishes. This is your workstation, Branson until Uncle Sam ships you out. We serve three meals a day to five hundred hungry G. I's so there is no time to waste. I need the utensils three times each day and I want them clean and ready." Gritting my teeth I plunged headlong into the work just as I had with my work on the farm. I suppose my anger gave me the energy to work at the frantic pace expected of me but after a day or so I realized that the anger did me no good and I had to calmly accept my lot in life. The greater part of my camp-mates were involved in battle training before embarkation to Korea. I understood that I too would be going for cooks and dishwashers were needed over there too. I made a request to see the commanding officer; I told him that I wanted to be a truck driver.

"When you get to Korea, Branson you might thank your lucky stars you are in the catering corps and not the infantry."

"I don't care Sir; I want to be a truck driver. I told them I wanted to be a driver when I first went to the draft."

"Have you any experience driving trucks, Branson?"

"Yes Sir." I saw the officer write something on my papers and then he said,

"Dismissed soldier." I returned to the mess kitchen convinced I would spend the rest of my time in the military up to my elbows in suds. It occurred to me at the time, that being up to the elbows in dishwater, is really no better than being up to my ass in beans. Disappointed in the outcome of the meeting I went back to washing dishes with a feeling of resignation that if this were my destiny I would do my best regardless.

When my comrades were considered battle ready, we were given twelve hours notice we were shipping out to Korea. All day and evening passes were cancelled. In the dark of night we were loaded on trucks then driven to an oceanfront dock near Los Angeles. As dawn broke we were loaded onto a troop ship packing full kit. Within minutes of the last man coming aboard, the ship slipped her moorings. On December fourteenth 1951 we were bound for Korea.

Hundreds of men stood at the ship's rails watching America become a series of gray colored bumps along the eastern horizon. It is my recollection that the mood of the men was one of bravado; they were going to kick the crap out of the enemy never once thinking that many of them would not see the gray lumps of receding America again. Aboard ship we were terribly crowded we had to lie on the floor to sleep. Hot meals were non-existent, we were issued army rations but hot coffee flowed in abundance. By nightfall of the same day the ocean had become rough and many of the men including myself began to experience seasickness. The flat bean landscape of Gage County had waved in the light summer winds, but this landscape of salty moving ocean my mind could not comprehend, nor my stomach tolerate.

Four day's out, the ship ran into a storm. Life now became a struggle to stand without clinging on to a part of the ship. Many claimed they wanted to die but of course no one did. By the time the ship tied up on the shores of Korea most of us were in such poor shape from seasickness we could not have fought our way out of a paper bag.

CHAPTER FOUR.

We were marched to a base camp where we were given a few days to recover. All of us were surprised how cold Korea was. Having left relatively warm California; we had wrongfully assumed it would be warm here too. In retrospect most of us were woefully ignorant of the people, the country, the customs and least of all the political reasons why we were here at all. We were there to fight for our country we were told from higher up. I could never for the life of me figure out how we could be fighting for our country, when we had left it so far behind.

We were called to parade on the morning of our fifth day in this strange land. Names were called out and those called were marched away to replace the casualties in the different units. There were only five of us left on the parade ground when finally I heard my name. I knew we five would be the kitchen helpers. A cigar-smoking captain with a long stogie clenched between his teeth informed us he was known in the motor pool as Smokey

Harrison. I heard the words "Motor Pool" there had to have been a mistake.

"You men are new to my unit. I'm proud of my boys. We run a tight ship we get the job done and get the equipment back to base no matter what. Which of you is Branson?"

"I am Sir."

"You have been assigned to drive one of our supply trucks Branson. I understand you have experience." My heart skipped a few beats. A truck. Me assigned a truck. I could hardly believe my ears. My head still spun when I responded automatically,

"Yes Sir. Thank You Sir."

"You other men will be assigned work in the motor pool repair section. Attention!" Captain Smokey Harrison marched us off to the motor pool. I felt that my feet barely touched the ground as I marched. I had no idea how my good fortune had come about but it had and now I would get to drive a truck for the army.

Captain Smokey handed the other men over to a sergeant in the repair shop then led me outside to a three axle truck with a canvas cover over the bed. She looked big and powerful large wheels with huge tires held her high off the ground. She wore camouflage colors of green brown and black. The half door bore the American star in white, with the numbers 2806 below in black.

"She's your baby now, Branson. Take care of her and she will take care of you. Because of the nature of the work you have to do, Branson I tend to be lenient with my drivers. Don't abuse the privilege or you will find yourself on latrine duty." I replied,

"I don't understand what you mean by the nature of

the work I will have to do, Sir."

"You will be delivering supplies to the front lines Branson, supplies that are vital to the front line guy's survival. You may find yourself dodging bullets both on the trip in and out. We are fighting an enemy who moves around all over the place. You are to get the goods to the front no matter what it takes and the same for getting back. I want that vehicle here for another load even if you have to drag the Goddamn thing home."

"I understand, Sir."

"There will be three of you going in the morning at first light. You will be in the rear position until you know the lay of the land. For Gods sake, Branson don't lose sight of the lead trucks or you may find yourself lost, alone and pretty damn soon dead meat. If you are not accustomed to this type of truck, jump aboard and familiarize yourself with it. Knowing how to handle her under fire hauling a load is critical."

"Yes Sir." I said excitedly. I sat in the driver's seat while Smokey Harrison stood on the running board pointing out the gear system and starting procedure.

"OK Branson, take me for a ride and show me what you know." I guess I must have done all right for he said, "She will be loaded and ready for you in the morning good luck on your first run."

Dawn broke cold. Frost covered everything so I wore my thick winter clothing with the earflaps sticking out from under my helmet. I met my two travel buddies and we pulled out of the base camp. Destruction reigned on each side of the road, flattened villages; tanks and trucks were burned out shells of their former glory. Jeeps in abundance lay in varying stages of destruction. We traveled about twenty miles without incident although the constant sound of gunfire disturbed the morning air. At the front line base station a horde of U.S. soldiers descended upon the supply trucks and within minute crates of ammo, grenades and mortars along with many jerry cans of fuel were placed on the ground and spirited away.

"There's a back load for you," the officer in charge told us. In the next few minutes I would receive my education on the horrors of war. The back load consisted of dead young soldiers, some with limbs blown off with landmines, others large pieces of their heads blown completely away. Others burned to cinders unrecognizable as humans. I staggered around to the front of 2806 and puked my guts as the bodies were loaded in my truck. I followed the two other trucks and Smokey Harrison came to me as we parked at the base camp.

"Rough morning Branson?" I nodded and unable to prevent it I puked again. "It may be hard to believe at this moment Branson, but it gets easier."

I am almost ashamed to say it but Captain Harrison was right, it did get easier. I had to set my mind against the horror of seeing our soldier's lives ended so far from home and amid such terrible carnage. One morning on our return trip the lead vehicle came across a blockage in the road.

"It's a trap!" The front driver yelled back at us. I slammed 2806 into reverse and hurtled backward at maximum throttle. I backed into some low bushes turned and shot forward again going back the way we had come. I glanced in my mirror and saw the other two trucks explode in flames. I caught a glimpse of Matt Varden leap from his cab and get mowed down by machine gun fire. There was absolutely nothing I could do to assist and I remembered Smokey Harrison's words. I found a new route through the maze of trails and made it back to base and reported the incident.

I now knew what the words 'you might be grateful you are in the catering corps meant.' It was a dangerous game I had wished myself into. By the same token infantrymen and many others were in a much more vulnerable position than I. A patrol went out to re-secure the road and the next morning I drove the lead truck to the front line. A heavy dose of bravado helped me get through the next few months. I developed the attitude that the enemy bastards were not going to get me. Early summer had come to the killing fields. The warmth had a twofold effect working conditions were much more comfortable, but new plant and foliage growth gave the enemy new hiding places for ambush. Truck number 2806 had become putty in my hands, I kept her finely tuned and she would go like the wind passing through danger zones. I think Smokey Harrison liked how I had turned out, he never said much but he used to give me encouraging nods. The kind of silent appreciation I would have expected my father back in Gage County to have given me but never did.

One morning in April of my time in Korea I drove fast with just a light back load of empty jerry cans. Traveling through open un-forested ground with no enemy in sight, I heard the whine of a projectile flying past my face and out the far side of the cab.

"Jeez that was"---- I never got the words out of my

mouth when my thighs exploded with a savage burning pain. I glanced down and saw a jagged hole in the door then blood began pouring from my thighs. Smokey Harrison's words hit my brain almost as fast. I had to get 2806 back to base. My legs no longer wanted to function, so I tore back the hand throttle, locked it at top speed and steered 2806 like a wild banshee in the direction of home base. Anyone witnessing my drive back in such a reckless and wild way would no doubt swear that I was as drunk as a skunk.

I careened into the compound without stopping at the security gate set back the hand throttle and jerked the gearshift into neutral and yarded on the handbrake causing 2806 to skid to a halt in a cloud of dust. Smokey Harrison must have seen or heard me coming for just before I lost consciousness I saw his face complete with cigar peering over the door. I saw him only once more after that when he came to see me in the field hospital. He stood over my bed with his cigar spilling ash over my blanket. He stuck out his hand and I pulled mine from under the blanket and took his.

"You did a great job Branson. A great job and I am proud to have had you as one of my drivers. You have driven your way into a ticket to Stateside. Uncle Sam is sending you home as soon as you are fit to travel." Captain Harrison turned on his heel and then he was gone. I began to think about home, something I hadn't done ʕ   ths. I thought about the praise Smokey
                    ffered me. To be praised for something I
                    ʼnderful. A whole new experience for me
                    ʼed. I felt I had worth. The thoughts led
                    of the Branson bean farm. Would my

father be proud of his son knowing I had cheated death in a foreign land? Would he welcome me home knowing his son was no longer a boy to be used and abused? Would he treat me as an equal if we worked the Branson land together?

The bullet had gone through my left leg and entered and exited the right. The exit site had mushroomed; causing a huge wound that would require a great deal of healing leaving me with a permanent limp. I asked for and received my carving kit. I could not abide idle hands so while my butt stayed firmly either in bed or in a wheel chair using pieces of ammo boxes I began to whittle a replica of truck number 2806. I started with the body, then the cab, carving the minutest details. By the time the army wanted to ship me Stateside I had it completed, right down to the tread on the six tires. I had a feeling that when my father heard the story of how the truck and I had been in the war together and how her high speed had in fact saved my life he would accept my gift gracefully and be proud of it.

The greater part of my wound had healed. The doctors said I would need considerable rehabilitation treatment to rebuild and get my shattered muscles to work. This work would be done back in the states. A huge military airplane with the lower half filled with coffins and the upper half, with wounded like myself left the killing fields of Korea far behind. We were going home.

The journey seemed to last forever, the aircraft was ice cold inside and the engine noise deafening. Despite the discomfort, our jubilation at coming home could not be dampened and when the big wheels scorched the California tarmac a weary cheer drowned out the r of the engines. A military ambulance delivered me to a rehab facility close to San Francisco. The place was loaded with the walking wounded and the non-walking, I knew I was one of the lucky ones I saw comrades with both legs gone, others with arms missing, still others with terrible head injuries. After three months of painful therapy I had learned to walk tolerably well although I had a pronounced limp in my right leg. Those of us able to get around unaided were given the freedom to go into San Francisco for evenings out and it was on such an evening I met Patsy Wallace.

Dressed in our uniforms, two friends and I were eating in a Chinese restaurant. The busy place had only a few seats left when two girls walked in. They looked around and it appeared they were about to leave when my fellow soldier, Wilf spoke to them,

"Come and join us, there is plenty of room at our table." The girls hesitated, spoke to each other and then agreed to share our table. Patsy, tall and slim wearing a simple but stunning cotton dress, white with large red roses gracing it and matching white shoes with tall heels, sat directly across from me. I could not take my eyes off her. Patsy was beautiful. Not Betty Grable type beautiful, but she had a kind of clean simple appearance that held me enchanted. Her blonde hair styled with a short cut reminiscent of a schoolgirl, framed a flawless face with high cheekbones and deep blue eyes that met mine with a perceived appreciation of my looks.

For the first time in my life I felt I might be handsome and even attractive, no longer the hillbilly boy of a year ago. It was not a feeling; I knew instinctively that, Patsy liked me. We gazed at each other across the table our eyes parting only when the menu thrust before her broke the line of vision. I am not a bright or educated man but I knew at that moment, Patsy would become a large part of my life just as surely as I would always limp. Not a word had yet passed between us, for my part none were needed and deep in my heart I had a feeling Patsy felt the same things as I.

Patsy put the menu down on the table.

"Try the number three it is very good. My name is Clement, Clem for short." I pointed at number three on the menu, Patsy moved her finger to the menu and our fingers touched.

"I'm Patsy Wallace. Really I am Patricia but I prefer Patsy." Our fingertips remained touching; they became a highway bridge to all manner of unspoken emotions dreams and desires. My heart swelled with feelings hitherto unknown, I wanted my lips to touch hers and I wanted my arms to hold her close to my body, my nostrils to find the scent of her hair and my cheek to feel the softness of hers. My foot found hers under the table and Patsy did not recoil but touched mine softly with her shoe toe. There was not a shred of doubt in my mind I had found that special someone who would enrich my life with love, tenderness and respect for who I am. The thing that had eluded me in life so far. I had a momentary mad notion to stand on the table and proclaim to the world that love had come to me embodied in the girl before me.

"The number three sounds good Clem." The sound of her voice thrilled me. Like the big organ in the church back in Gage County it induced a feeling of awe and reverence. Such simple words yet to me saying so much.

"Have you been drafted and going overseas to Korea?" Patsy asked.

"No, Patsy I have just recently come back from over there as have my two friends."

"Then are you on leave, Clem?"

No. We are home to stay; we have all caught bullets in one place or the other so Uncle Sam doesn't need us any more. We are staying in the rehab hospital until the doctors feel we are well enough to resume our lives in the civilian world."

"Where did you get injured Clem?"

"I caught it in my thighs. But I am doing O.K. I can walk all right although they say I will always limp a bit." Patsy extended her hand across the table and took my hand in hers; a lump came to my throat recognizing that Patsy cared. I knew she shared my pain but knowing it made it all seem as nothing, making it all worthwhile.

"Tell me about you Patsy? Do you live with your parents? Were you born in San Francisco?"

"I will tell you all about myself, Clem but not now, not here. Perhaps you will walk with me after we have eaten?" The raw power of 2806 could not have held me back from walking with Patsy. I watched every sweet movement of her mouth as she ate her meal and her gaze met mine as she raised her eyes from the plate. There was no embarrassment, no awkward moments, just two people who had found each other in a world of drifting souls looking for a place to land. After we had all finished, Patsy's friend, astutely recognizing what had happened between Patsy and I, made an excuse about having to get home, left us and went to catch a bus. My two companions went in search of a tavern.

Patsy and I wandered through Chinatown looking in the store windows our hands each finding the other's just as naturally as though they had always belonged there.

"You were going to tell me about yourself Patsy?"

"I come from humble beginnings Clem. My folks were basically what folks call white trash. We lived in a decrepit old trailer house in West Virginia. My daddy worked in a coal mine when he wasn't drinking. Mother had a part time job house cleaning for a few folks in the area having money. I remember her as being just as eager as daddy to get into the drink. Most weekends were a kind of nightmare for me, I remember mother would not bother making meals when she was on the booze then daddy would get angry and slap her around. The fighting always frightened me and I would hide under my bed until it died down or they went to sleep. Lots of weekends I had very little to eat, sometimes I would find a potato or a carrot or two if I was lucky maybe even some bread slices and I would spread them with ketchup.

When they sent me to school I often went hungry, but there were other white trash children in the same boat. Thinking back I suppose we thought this was normal and despite our young age we supported each other. At the age of eight I became an orphan. My parents were out drinking at a tavern on the outskirts of town, my daddy driving his beat up old Model A Ford on the way home missed a curve and drove deep into the river in spring flood. It was June when the roof of the car became visible; they found my folks sitting bolt upright in the car slowly decomposing. Of course by then I had been sent by the county to live with my grandmother.

Gran always figured it had been the demon drink

that had done them in and landed me in her lap and of course she turned out to be correct. Gran was my mother's mother and she told me many times how she had warned my mother not to marry the Wallace boy, but she went ahead, ignored the advice and paid the ultimate price.

Life with gran was a different kettle of fish. She always had a full table and she had a kindly way about her but she expected complete obedience. That is not to say she was overly strict, she wasn't, I had a fair amount of freedom to play and be with my friends. I lived with gran until I reached the age of seventeen. For a year she had been getting progressively weaker and unable to manage. I tried to get her to see a doctor but Gran was adamant.

"I've lived three score years and ten without a nosey doctor and I won't have one now!" she would say to me. Well gran just faded away from this world one night, peacefully and without fanfare. She left me her meagre savings and I came out to San Francisco to start life with a clean slate.

You may think this is odd, Clem I have never told my story to anyone before, but I have a distinct feeling you are the one person who will not judge me for my beginnings. Now tell me about you, Clem?"

I felt just as, Patsy did, that I could tell her the story of my life without any fear of her rejecting me or judging me, I knew instinctively my feelings were safe with Patsy. Like her I began at the beginning and ending with me here holding her hand. We had walked and talked the evening away and I had to get the bus back to the rehab hospital. We arranged to meet the following night and

Patsy offered me her lips as my bus arrived. No dessert. No candy, nothing in my life had ever tasted so sweet. A sweetness I knew that I could never get my fill of. I saw nothing out of the bus window. I do not remember the walk to the rehab place. My mind was consumed by her kiss. Nothing else in the world mattered.

My rehabilitation exercises the next day dragged on interminably, I willed every minute to be gone so I could be with, Patsy. A feeling deep in my chest brought on by desire to touch, Patsy again, joined the pain of my spirit having finally found a place to rest and yearning to be there. We met at the appointed place and our lips converged not in a gentle welcoming touch, but in a strong sensual urge apparent in each of us. The force I now know as love; had awakened in us with a clamour that would not be ignored. I recognized this was the emotion lacking in my experiences getting laid as a new recruit in a stumbling attempt to prove my manhood. My feelings for, Patsy were of a much higher plane. I wanted to encircle her in my arms, to make her feel safe, loved and to feel her love in return. To lie with her, each trusting the other completely, to be naked and unembarrassed, to feel the softness of her skin against mine and eventually to be as one in mind body and spirit.

You may think of me as a fool, for I asked Patsy, to marry me before we had even left the bus stop. We had known each other less than twenty-four hours and yet without any hesitation, Patsy agreed. Military protocol required I obtain permission to marry. My superiors granted my request, but until my rehabilitation therapy had been completed I would be required to continue living at the hospital. Patsy and I endured the agony of withholding our powerful urges to become lovers in the physical sense. Patsy was much stronger than I, wishing to give herself to me only after our wedding. My strong sexual urges constantly denied, brought physical discomfort to my private parts, the doctor said that under the circumstances my complaint was absolutely normal. We were allowed to marry the week before my discharge from rehab. We had a simple civic ceremony with, Patsy wearing the pretty dress she had worn the night we met. I had the creases in my uniform pressed to razor edges and my boots shone like mirrors. With a traditional honeymoon being out of the question we would consummate our love in Patsy's tiny apartment. Every second of every minute of our first wondrous lovemaking is etched forever in my brain. Every dream, every wish and desire came to fruition. The empty cup of my self worth overflowed. My heart, my soul, my very being had found safe haven in Patsy's arms. We did not leave our love nest for a full night and day. However the pressures of life outside the apartment door dictated that we fly back to earth from the clouds we had been suspended in.

"Will you be going back to the bean farm Clem?"

"Not if it means you will not be there with me."

"I will go anywhere you go Clem Branson. I will work alongside you if you want to return, after all, will not the farm be yours one day?"

"I had never thought of it before, but yes it will likely be mine when father dies. My concern is for you, Patsy you have tasted city life here in San Francisco. Could you adjust to the life on a Gage County bean farm?"

"With you at my side, Clem I could live anywhere.

Besides life will be different if you go back to the farm. You are your own man now Clem Branson, having escaped from under your father's thumb; you will no longer allow him to dominate you. He has to pay you wages and respect your ideas. If he does not give you these things, the road leads away from the farm just as surely as it does to it."

"You are the smartest person I know, Patsy Branson. You are right; if father misbehaves toward us, we will up and leave. I know how to grow good beans and I know how to drive trucks. With you at my side I believe I can make a living and look after us well enough. If you are sure you are ok with it, we will go back to Gage County. How much notice do you have to give at your job with the phone company?"

"Just seven working days I can hand it in tomorrow if you wish then we could leave the following week."

"I'll check tomorrow. I think the army will pay my train fare back to Gage County, there will just be yours to find. Now come back to bed. I can't bear to not have you next to me."

In the mornings before my therapy began and during my lunch periods I carved a small statue of Patsy, I carved it with the greatest of care and with overwhelming love in my heart. A tear came to her eye when I presented it to her.

"No one has ever made anything especially for me before. Thank you Clem." Not since I had made the little dove for Eliza and Amos, had I felt such pride in my ability. Patsy held and fondled the statue in her hands alternating her smile between it and I. My self esteem grew in leaps and bounds. Patsy opened her arms for me and I entered them. Leading me to her single bed she showed her appreciation for my gift with one of her own.

Later that night as I lay in my cot at the rehab hospital, it occurred to me that I had not contacted my father since the day I left the farm. I felt I should advise him I would soon be coming home. I borrowed a notepad and pen from the soldier in the next bed. I sat for ages trying to write a letter to my father but I could not find the words to put to paper. The blank page seemed like a mirror and father's sour face stared back at me. I did not know how I could write when he barely ever spoke to me and he certainly had never listened to me.

Then I remembered Liza and Amos. I would write the letter to Liza and she could tell him the news. I didn't know for sure of course but I didn't think Liza would let father browbeat her, in my opinion she had way too much character for that. I began to write.

> *Dear Liza and Amos how are you.*
> *I have been to Korea and I got to drive trucks.*
> *I got shot in the leg but I'm ok, just limp a bit.*
> *The army doesn't need me any more so I am*
> *coming home next week. I met a girl called Patsy*
> *We are married and she will be coming with me.*
> *Your friend Clement Branson.*

I bought a stamp and put the letter in the mail. Patsy arranged for her friend Margery to take over her apartment on the day we left for Gage County. We would be able to travel light, Patsy with one large suitcase and I with my kitbag and the carton containing the model of

2806 for my father. After what had seemed an eternity, my release from the rehab hospital came through along with my travel documents.

Patsy and I were to catch the morning eastbound train. We stood together holding hands with our luggage on the ground beside us; we were embarking on a new and wonderful life together. I was overjoyed at the prospect at never having to be parted from Patsy but yet deep down in my gut I had an unexplainable feeling of foreboding. As we listened, straining to hear the sound of the approaching train, I wondered is it because I did not know how my father would greet us or that deep down I still feared him. I kept my feelings to myself I did not want, Patsy to be disturbed by them. So far as she knew we were setting off on the adventure of a love filled life together. I drew in a deep breath and resolved that my father would not be allowed to come between us in any way. I would stand up to him. I would work alongside him but I would not allow him to dominate me and I most certainly not allow him to treat Patsy the way he had my mother. Out on the horizon the bright headlight of the locomotive beamed what appeared to me to be an omen of a bright life for, Patsy and I. The clanking bell and hissing steam on its arrival indicated the start of it.

We found our seats and settled down for the long journey to Gage County. We sat holding hands watching the world slip by our window, we passed through grotty back streets of towns, through cacti infested desert and fields of wheat, dairy cattle, vegetables and fruit orchards. With Patsy at my side all this seemed fresh and new quite unlike my previous journey on this same line

84

dressed in my farm clothes and feeling totally alienated and afraid. Now as passengers passed down the train seeing me in my smart uniform, they gave me nods of respect. As we walked to the dining car they saw my limp and gave understanding smiles, they seemed to understand that I had been wounded in the service of my country. I felt proud, but not so proud as when Patsy sat across the dining table from me her radiance filling me with warmth and love.

We slept the night away sitting up, with arms locked around each other the only comfort either of us needed. Below the railcar the clatter of wheels on steel rail brought us ever closer to Gage County. In the state between sleep and wakefulness I wondered about some of my fellow wounded soldiers and how their mother's and father's would greet them on their homecoming, I imagined tears of relief and joy loving embraces. Father's so grateful their son had returned that they held on to them with bone crushing hugs and mother's weeping tears of utter joy that the flesh of her flesh had returned to her. The semi dream state led me on to the homecoming I expected. A huge sob coming from deep inside woke both Patsy and I.

"What is it, Clem?" She enquired obviously concerned.

"I'm sorry, Patsy, I was just thinking about my mother and how she would have welcomed me home were she still alive. It was like a dream that I knew would never come true." Patsy held me close and I knew she understood no further explanation was necessary.

At noon the train entered the rolling landscape of Gage County bean fields. Bean flowers of blues and shades of purple and white waved like the Pacific Ocean in the early summer breeze. Off in the distance I saw against the skyline the familiar outline of the bean storage elevators, in an odd way they seemed to be welcoming me home.

"We are here, Patsy my love," I said standing to get our luggage ready to alight from the train. With a squeal of brakes followed by silence we had arrived. We were the only passengers to get off and with a shriek of the whistle and a clanging of the bell; we were alone on the station platform. I looked to see if my father had come to meet us. He had not and as usual I gave him the benefit of the doubt, telling myself he may not have known which train to meet. Outside the station one of the town's two taxis waited hopefully for a fare.

We loaded our luggage into the cavernous trunk of the 1947 Chrysler and told the driver where we needed to go. As we drove through the farm gate I saw my father step out of the house onto the porch. I gripped Patsy's hand and the thought struck me like a rock hurled at my head that thus far in my life, I had never seen my father smile.

CHAPTER FIVE.

The taxi lurched to a stop sending a small dust cloud swirling into the air. The driver got out retrieved our luggage from the trunk, held out his hand for the fare then left. The car sent up a second dust cloud which followed him out to the road. I had the oddest feeling that the driver hadn't wanted to be on Branson land a moment longer than necessary.

Father stood on the porch, hands on hips, his hat hiding his eyes from our view his patched and grubby overalls instantly reminded me of myself the day I left the Branson bean farm to go to the army. I approached the porch steps holding Patsy's hand and looked up into my father's face. Not even a trace of a smile of welcome did I see but I did see his mean little mouth quiver and I knew he had something to say, but I also knew it wasn't 'welcome home son.'

"I wrote to Liza. Did she tell you I would be coming home and that I would be bringing my wife back with me?" Father nodded.

"Are you proper church wed?" he asked accusingly. I saw no point in telling him Patsy and I had been married in a civil ceremony, for I knew he would go off the rails if he thought otherwise.

"Yes Father. This is my bride, Patsy." His rat-like eyes searched, Patsy up and down as though she were a stray cat begging for a home. "Where are Amos and Liza Father, out in the fields?"

"I let them go after she told me you were coming back. Aint no point in paying for help I no longer needed." Father turned to go back into the house. Anger began to swiftly rise in my breast. I hadn't expected much of a welcome from him but he had not said hello or acknowledged Patsy with even a cursory wave of his hand. He had fired Amos and Liza probably expecting me to continue the subservient role I had before leaving.

"Stop right there!" I yelled at him. "Things are not going to be as they were before I left! I am not the same person you let walk away from this farm like a pauper or a circus clown! If Patsy and I are to stay on this Goddamn bean farm we have to be respected and dealt with properly." I saw that my use of the word Goddamn shocked him as his mean little mouth dropped open. "I will no longer be your unpaid slave Father. If Patsy and I are to stay, I insist on being paid wages and if Patsy helps out in the fields you will damn well pay her too. Above all you will treat her with the dignity and respect she deserves."

I saw that my use of words he considered profane offended him and were having great effect. I think he had expected I would come meekly home and things would go on as before. His jaw dropped lower and lower in muted shock. Having started as I meant to go on, I continued.

"Patsy is my wife Father. I love her! If you have any Goddamn idea what love is and I doubt that you do, any disrespect you show to Patsy is disrespect for me and I will not tolerate it. We agreed before coming back here if you are rude, or attempt to treat either of us badly we would walk away from this place and never come back! That's not a threat Father; it's a fucking promise. I have learned new skills while away and I don't need you and your Jesus freak attitude or this asshole bean farm to make a Goddamn living!"

I could tell my father was shocked almost out of his boots. I really wasn't sure whether it was my use of profanity or my surprise demands, but right now at this minute I didn't give a damn. I felt good inside; I had refused to be submissive. I had asserted my self and that of Patsy's position as my beloved wife. It may have been my appearance dressed with my uniform looking sharp and pressed, in contrast with his appalling attire that gave me the position of superiority over father, but more likely it was my attitude that I would no longer accept his dictates. Patsy gripped my hand; I knew instinctively she was proud of me.

Father stood stock still mouth agape his rat-like eyes open wide, the first time I had ever seen them that way. He reacted as he had done in earlier days. He lunged at me no doubt intending to give me a thrashing, but the old fool hadn't reckoned with my army hand-to-hand fight training. I dropped my kitbag on the ground and floored father with my first punch. He lay in the Gage County dust with blood streaming from his nose. His hat lay off to the side and I saw him lying at my feet staring up at me shocked and surprised like a beaten cur.

I realized what a pathetic little man father really was. This pitiful creature that had spread hate fear and loathing to his own family I felt he had done so to cover his own inadequacies. This wretched man knew nothing of love as Patsy and I knew love. I realized too that mother had probably died needlessly as a result of his tyranny and forced labor. I resisted the strong urge to put my highly polished boots to his ribs for the longer I stared the more pathetic he appeared. I backed away and re-took Patsy's hand.

"That's enough, Clem. I don't think he will try to harm you anymore. My God you sure were not kidding when you said what a miserable man your father was." I knew that Patsy disliked violence as much as I, but I felt she understood the showdown was inevitable and necessary given the circumstances.

Father slowly regained his feet. With my fist clenched I was more than ready should he think he could still dominate me. Noting it he turned away and picked up his hat. He was beaten and humiliated and I had the feeling he would never try to strike me again. With his shoulders sloping forward and his head bowed he walked up the porch steps then into the house without a single word leaving his lips.

"Well. Do we stay or do we leave?" Patsy asked.

"Frankly Patsy, I don't think he will give us any trouble from now on. I'm sure he knows he cannot treat me as he used to do. He is aware now that I will not take it. He knows I will thump him again or we will up and leave as we agreed. We have to negotiate the terms of employment, the remuneration and the boundaries of privacy that must be set for us. With your agreement we can enter the house and state our terms, but if you do not feel you can live here we can head out of the gate right now and thumb a ride into town."

"I've put up with miserable people before in my life Clem. For your sake I will put up with your father so long as there are some solid ground rules. But like you say if he becomes unbearable we can hightail it out of here and go back to San Francisco or Chicago or even New York."

"Then let's go in and try to make peace and set the rules." We picked up our luggage and stepped into the kitchen. I had forgotten how disgustingly grotty the farm kitchen looked. After working in military kitchens where cleanliness was king, this place looked almost like a refuse dump. Forty-year-old paint had forty years of kitchen frying fat stuck to it. Spilled food coated the stove, the sink equally filthy, had gray and stained cleaning cloths hanging over the edge and the dishes from father's latest meals sat unwashed in the bottom. A pail of ashes stood un-emptied by the stove and the floor hadn't seen a scrub brush since the day Liza had left.

I glanced at Patsy and saw she was taking in the mess no doubt wondering where she would begin the mammoth task of cleaning it up.

"There are things we have to talk about Father." He sat blankly staring into the stove firebox. He did not speak but he nodded and it became plain that it would be I doing most of the talking.

"Father you may not like to hear this but this house is a pigsty! I will work with Patsy to clean it up and we will repaint the rooms. This is no fit place for my wife to be working or living in. You are to pay us a reasonable remuneration for our work, both of us. We wish to have our privacy guaranteed and our rights respected. In return we will help to run the Branson Farm. Saturday will be our day off each week except at harvest time. Do we understand each other?"

Father nodded but did not raise his face to look at me.

"*What about church on Sundays. Will you be going?*" He asked. I looked at Patsy it was something we had not discussed. She gave a quick shake of her head.

"No." I answered and father to my surprise did not argue. Feeling much calmer now I said,

"I don't know if Liza told you Father but the army sent me to Korea, it's over the ocean a long way from America. Over there I was given the job of driving a big supply truck. The army liked the way I worked and I enjoyed the job even though sometimes it was dangerous. One day a big bullet came through the cab door and passed through both of my legs. The right leg came off worst and as a result I will always have a limp. It might slow me down a little but I can still do a hard day's work. Any way Father, while I recuperated in the hospital over there in Korea, I made this for you it's an accurate replica of my truck, number 2806. I carved it out of ammo boxes and stained it with juice from walnut husks. I handed him the carton and Patsy and I watched him unwrap it. He turned it around in his hands, gave a cursory nod then placed the model on the stove plate warming rack.

"Which will be our room," Patsy whispered to me.

"Let's go look." I answered. My old room had a

sagging single bed and my room had not been cleaned since I had occupied it. The spare room had no bed in it and I remembered it had been moved to the tractor shed for Liza and Amos. I took Patsy's hand and we left to go and look in the outbuilding where Liza and her husband had lived. Upon opening the door I was amazed, the place was much cleaner than the house. Liza had made it into a home and the bed had been left neatly made with clean sheets.

"Let's stay here, Clem at least until we get the house cleaned up properly. I will feel much more comfortable here than in the house with your miserable father."

"So will I Patsy, so will I." I went back to the house to bring our luggage and as I stepped into the kitchen I saw the stove firebox burning brightly with the model of 2806 surrounded by consuming flames, my father watching it burn. I knew at that moment that I would never have my father's love or approval; any chance of it soared up the stove flue and into the Gage County air.

The old feeling of wanting to cry at my father's actions came to me for just a second but I fought it off. I made an instant decision that I would never allow him to hurt me again. I went back to Patsy in the old tractor shed we climbed between the sheets and slept a tired sleep. In the predawn light we made love surrounded by the sweet perfume of a million bean flowers.

We went to the house where Patsy and I together made breakfast for all of us. When father had finished his Morning Prayer session and we had cleaned the dishes, I told father,

"Patsy and I are going into town. I have to buy work clothes; for I am proud of my uniform I will not sully it by wearing it for farm work. We are also going to buy cleaning supplies and paint for the kitchen and the back bedroom. If you have a list of supplies we will need I can pick them up at the same time."

Father nodded agreement and reached for a coffee can, out of which he produced a wad of paper money. He counted out fifty dollars and wordlessly handed it to me. I was shocked to say the least, firstly I had no idea he kept a stash of cash in the house and secondly that he handed me the money with no admonitions to spend it frugally. Thirdly he surprised me by not insisting that cleaning and painting were an unnecessary waste of money.

Patsy went to change her dress and I got a spare blanket to cover the bare springs on the truck's passenger seat. I looked at the disgusting collection of rubbish and dried mud in the cab and began to clean it up for my lovely Patsy to ride in with me. She emerged from the tractor shed wearing a thin cotton dress I had never seen her in before, her hair freshly brushed, gleamed in the Gage County morning sun. Patsy looked so beautiful and radiant it almost took my breath away. I stood by the truck door with my arms open wide for her, she entered them and our lips met and the desire to make love with her right here and now surged within me. From the corner of my eye I saw father observing us from the porch pretending not to notice.

I opened the door to my princess's coach and as she climbed in and sat my hand trailed down her shapely leg, Patsy smiled at me and I knew she wanted me too. The old International burst into dubious life with a puff of blue smoke and a swirl of dust accompanied us as we rolled out of the Branson bean farm gate. The bean crops all around us were about three feet high, dark green and covered in multi-shaded flowers.

"Pull over where it is safe to park, Clem I want to stroll among the beans."

Out of sight of the farm buildings I pulled over at a wide spot on the roadside. Patsy alighted, picked up the blanket and walked into the unfenced field. I turned off the engine and followed her. She lay the blanket down amid the bean plants and beckoned me to sit with her, within seconds we were naked and writhing in impassioned lovemaking. The warm morning sun beaming down on our unclothed bodies added a whole new dimension to our expressions of love. With our immediate passion spent we lay panting and relaxed as the sun dried the sweat from our skin.

"I'm glad I came to Gage County with you Clem Branson," Patsy whispered in my ear. I turned onto my side and kissed her magnificent breasts,

"And I'm glad you came with me," I replied.

At the bean co-op general store I bought overalls and work shirts that fit me properly, no longer would I go round looking like a circus clown, I had developed way to much pride in myself for that. I bought sturdy work boots and polish to take care of them. Patsy found some loose hanging cheap cotton dresses for working around the house and farm then she chose stout walking shoes for work.

"I won't be found dead wearing farmers boots," she declared. Together we chose two gallons of bright yellow paint for the kitchen and a rose pink flat paint for the back bedroom, which would be ours when we moved into the house. Patsy found some materiel to make new curtains for our room a similar shade of pink with a red rose print. By the time we had bought grocery and cleaning supplies and gassed up the truck the fifty dollars had all been spent, plus I put twelve dollars on the Branson co-op account.

It took two days of Patsy and I cleaning to get all the accumulated grime out of the kitchen, finally it awaited the new coat of paint. Within twenty-four hours the linoleum had been cleaned up and the room was transformed into a bright place to work and eat. Patsy's radiance had left its mark on the Branson house within days of her arrival. Next we worked on the back bedroom and with the double bed from the tractor shed installed, it became our special and private place. On warm nights we would lie naked on the bed taking in the perfume of bean flowers and expressing our boundless love for each other with our bodies.

Soon long pods filled with quality beans replaced the bean flowers. Father kept out of our way for the most part, Patsy produced tasty meals and I helped her to work the garden, then we worked side by side preserving the produce in mason jars. When bean harvesting began Patsy helped us. Working in the heat of day, Patsy took to just wearing her thin cotton dresses without her bra I loved to see her this way with the darkness of her nipples showing through. It reminded me constantly of why I loved her so much.

"Clem," she confided in me. "Your father keeps staring at my breasts he is not even subtle, he is leering at me I can sense it. He seems to come closer just so he can see through my dress." I had never thought of my father, as being a sexually interested person there had never been any indication of it in the past.

"Perhaps you should go back to wearing your bra, Patsy I love to see you without it but perhaps father finds it disturbing."

"Then I shall Clem."

We had a load of beans to be delivered to the bean co-op elevator. Often Patsy would come with me to town just for a change of scenery and also that we had some time by ourselves. But this day Patsy was busy canning our pea crop from the garden and declined.

"See you when you get back, Clem," she said contentedly. I waited my turn to unload and weigh at the elevator then I set off back to the farm. About a quarter mile from our gate a saw a person running headlong down the road toward me. As I drew closer I saw it was Patsy her hair all askew and with her dress in tatters. Even from the truck cab I could see she had on no underwear. I jammed on the brakes and shouted,

"Patsy! What's the matter Patsy?" Now I could see tears streaming down her cheeks. She kept on running as she passed the truck.

"Your father raped me!" She shouted breathlessly.

"Stop and tell me what happened Patsy?"

"Your father raped me," she yelled back as she kept on running away from me. I began to run after her, it was obvious she needed help to calm down and tell me in detail what had occurred. My accursed war wound would not let me keep pace with Patsy let alone gain on her. I knew the only way I could catch up with her was in the truck. I ran back jumped in the cab and went in search of a wide spot where I could turn the Goddamn thing around. Once I had, I came roaring down the road with blue smoke pouring from the protesting engine but Patsy was nowhere in sight. She must have left the road and gone cross-country through the harvested bean fields.

A terrible panic began to grow in my breast. Patsy the one person in my life whom I loved and unreservedly loved me in return had run away. I could not go after her for I had no idea where she may have left the road, or even which direction she might head. I drove up and down but saw no sign of her. My panic began to turn to anger. It was anger such, as I have never known. It started at my groin and filled my body right up to my throat. My temples were desperate to explode and there was an intense pressure behind my eyes. My fingers gripped the steering wheel almost sufficient to melt the cracked Bakelite.

I turned the truck around and headed for the farm. I swear that old piece of shit truck never had traveled so fast before. I demolished a gatepost on my way into the yard jumped out while the truck still rolled for I had no concern on where it might end up. As I leapt up the three steps to the porch I saw the truck demolish the tractor shed. Nothing mattered. My father stood by the stove with that I am holier than thou look in his beady eyes and that's when I grabbed the carving knife and thrust it deep into his hateful body.

Looking back upon that day so long ago, a kind of madness held me completely in its grip. No longer was he Jed Branson. He had become as one of the enemy in Korea where human life and blood were as meaningless as spilled sewage. I stared down at my father's corpse sorry there was nothing else I could do to hurt the son-of-a-bitch any more. Frankly I thought of gutting him like some of our soldiers had been done in Korea. I didn't, my anger began to subside and I thought better of it. My only regret about my actions was that my father didn't live long enough to suffer more from my fury. Had I the opportunity to live that day again I would kill him slowly inch by inch and have him know and suffer the pain he had caused his son and was about to heap more of it upon me.

I went outside and sat on the porch with my legs dangling over the edge. Taking deep breaths my heart rate began to come down and my sanity slowly returned. I had murdered my father. It was all over but the consequences and there would be serious legal consequences. The loss of Patsy made all of them seem minor inconveniences compared to her leaving me. Patsy meant everything. Without her there was nothing. She formed part of my heart and part of my soul we were one, not only in the physical sense during lovemaking but our two beings made each of the other a whole person. We had been as two leaves floating on the still pond of life we had miraculously found each other and destiny had decreed we would be joined until we faded away. But my rotten father had taken away that for which I lived.

Calmer now, I had to make some realistic decisions. I could drag his body and force it under the effluent in the outdoor pit toilet, it could rot there and the smell would be masked by the existing odour of the pit. Since father didn't often go to town except for church it might be fairly easy to explain his absence. Or, I could bury him in the newly plowed bean field after dark, the newly disturbed soil would tell no tales.

Unfortunately for me, mother had brought me up to have a conscience. I could do neither of those things. I had to do the honorable thing and report my actions to the Sheriffs department in town. I felt if I explained the circumstances truthfully the state would have compassion and treat me lightly and decently. After all had I not just returned as a wounded Korean War veteran? My conscience went to battle with the realization that I would be punished for my crime. It might mean that I would never see Patsy again, but the same scenario existed even if I disposed of father's body my self and kept his murder a secret. For I had no idea where I might begin to look for Patsy, she may have fled to a big city.

I made a small decision for now. I would wait right here until dark just in case Patsy decided to come back looking for me, then we could make the final decision between us. The prevailing winds brought storm clouds over Gage County that evening and darkness arrived earlier than usual. I rose from the porch and went inside and turned on the light, the body laid cold and stiff like the hog we killed every year. His blood had congealed in dark pools; his shirt and overalls were blackened with dried blood. Had I witnessed this scene before I went overseas and saw all the carnage I might have felt nauseous, but I felt no more emotion about his slaughter than if my father had been one of the bean silo rats.

I walked back outside to find out what had happened to the truck, for the last time I saw it the thing was hurtling through the tractor shed wall. It had stalled when the wheels struck the concrete footing and had actually suffered very little damage. I backed it out into the yard then went into the house to change into my uniform. I wanted to look my best when I turned myself in to the law. I checked the angle of my hat gave my boots a final buffing and left the house with the lights burning. I drove slowly towards town just in case Patsy had recovered from her trauma and was returning to me on the road. Had she been, there would have been a dramatic change in my plans but fate had decreed it was not to be. I parked in front of the Sheriff's office and went inside.

"I want to see Sheriff Coltrane?" I asked.

"He's gone home soldier, can I help?"

"No thank you sir, I want to talk to Sheriff Coltrane?"

"Then you had better come back in the morning soldier he comes in at eight. What is this about?"

"Murder. But I only want to speak with Mr. Coltrane about it."

"Whose murder?"

"My father's."

"Take a seat soldier. I will call the sheriff at home. You had better not be pulling our legs you can be charged with mischief." Twenty minutes later sheriff Coltrane strode into the office looking completely un-amused at having his dinner interrupted. The deputy pointed him in my direction.

"You are here to report a murder soldier? Step into my office." I followed him in and he sat behind a desk and motioned me to sit in front.

"Now soldier what is your name and why did you insist on talking only to me?"

"My name is Clement Branson sir. I wanted to speak with you because you have a reputation in this area of being a good and fair man."

"All my deputies are fair and decent men Mr. Branson. Now what is this all about?"

"I have killed my father sir, this afternoon in our farmhouse."

"Is your father the Branson who has a bean farm out on valley road, the religious fellow?"

"Yes sir."

"Why and how did you kill your father, Clement?"

"I stabbed him with our carving knife sir. He raped my wife Patsy while I went to town with a load of beans to the elevator."

"Where is Patsy now Clement?"

"She has run away sir. I found her running from the farm crying and with her clothing torn. With my war wound I couldn't catch up to her running, she must have taken off across country for even with the truck I couldn't catch up or find her."

"Then how do you know your father raped her?"

"She told me, as she ran past the truck when I stopped on the road"

"Where is the body now Clement?"

"Still on the kitchen floor where he fell when I stabbed him."

"Why did you stab him Clement would in not have been better to have the law handle the situation?"

"I came to you Sheriff Coltrane because I thought you would understand. I love, Patsy more than anything in this world. My father has always been mean and cruel toward me and when I brought Patsy my wife back to the farm to live with me after the army didn't want me anymore, I think he bitterly resented her and I think he raped her simply to hurt me. I was more hurt than I have ever been in my life before and the hurt turned to anger then fury when my father grinned at me as I strode into the house, I lost control Sheriff and I picked up the knife and stuck him just like the army showed us. What I am trying to say sir is that I am not a bad man, but a man who has been driven to extremes by a cruel unfeeling father. I know I have done wrong, but I cannot undo it and I am hoping you will understand and be lenient with me."

"I appreciate your putting your trust in me Clement, but the fact is any lenience is the jurisdiction of the courts. I will be as helpful as I can be under the circumstances but your fate is quite out of my hands. Now we had best go out to the farm and have a look at things, is that your truck parked out front?"

"Yes sir."

"Then you had better drive it back to the farm and I and one of my deputies will follow you in a police car." The sheriff spoke to a deputy and made a couple of short phone calls then he said,

"O.K. son. Let's go." I drove out to the farm with a police car and an ambulance following. I parked the truck in the barn for I figured it would not be going anywhere for a while. I led the sheriff and his deputy into the house and pointed to father's body. I saw with some degree of surprise that during the process of rigor mortis setting in, father's face had taken on the merest hint of a smile. His dead unfeeling eyes seemed to stare directly into my own. They were accusing eyes. Eyes that seemed to express the last word.

"Sit down at the table Clement." The sheriff ordered. The deputy took photographs of the kitchen and the body then the ambulance men covered it after laying him on a stretcher. They took the body away. That was the last I ever saw of my father.

"Give me your hands," the sheriff demanded. "I have to do this Clement," he said as placed handcuffs around my wrists. Then he walked me out to the police car and locked me in the back seat.

"Sir," I asked. "There are two things in the back bedroom I would like to take with me. One is a small carving of my wife Patsy, the other a small box of carving tools my mother gave to me before she died."

"O.K. Clement. But you must realize that you will not be able to have the tools with you as they could become weapons, but they can be held with your personal possessions along with your uniform when you get your prison garb."

"Thank you sir." No further words passed between the sheriff and I until we reached his office. He led me in through the back door and once inside he said,

"Clement Branson I am charging you with the murder of Jed Branson a resident of Gage County." He handed me over to a different deputy who took me to a cell, told me to strip and step into a prison jumpsuit. The door clanged shut and my life of incarceration began. The next morning after a sleepless night wondering where Patsy might have gone, if she was safe and if I would ever see her again, the deputy took me in ankle chains and handcuffs before a judge.

"How do you plead?" He asked after hearing the charge against me. I replied

"Guilty but I did it under extreme provocation."

"Do you have an attorney Mr. Branson?"

"No your honour. I do not know any attorneys."

"Then the court will appoint you one and you will be tried on the charge of murder in thirty days."

The deputy led me back to my cell where I spent the next thirty days alone except for the occasional drunk they would put in the cell next to me. I suppose the loneliness might affect some people, but I had grown up with it, so it didn't bother me to any great degree. The Sheriff kept me supplied with books and magazines also providing me with quite good meals.

The court appointed attorney came to see me to prepare my case. He appeared to be very old, his clothes hung from his frame suggesting he had once been a large robust man now shrinking into a shadow of his former self. A few wisps of white hair circled his shiny baldhead and his eyes took on the gray glassy appearance that most old people seemed to develop. Deep wrinkles surrounded his chin.

"I'm Franklin Dale your court appointed attorney," he said in greeting. "Now young man, tell me exactly what happened so I can prepare your defense." I told Mr. Dale how I had encountered Patsy running down the road and that she had said my father had raped her, how I lost my self-control and went to the farm and killed my father.

"The French would call this a crime of passion Mr. Branson, in America we do not have it on our law books, but I will do my best to beg the court's understanding and leniency given the circumstances. It will not be easy since you have already pleaded guilty."

I didn't see Franklin Dale again until I stood in the courtroom for my trial.

"We are up against, Abe Clark a young eager beaver district attorney running for re-election Mr. Branson. He could be a formidable adversary." Franklin Dale whispered. The date of my trial arrived and the court clerk read the charge against me. Abe Clark stood looking at me as though I were dirt, just the way my father had done.

"Ladies and gentlemen of the jury in the prisoners box sits a heinous criminal. So heinous is he, that he murdered his own father. An unarmed God-fearing farmer who had lovingly raised his son and provided a home for he and his wife and had given him employment. The State will prove the prisoner callously murdered his father so that he could inherit the farm using a pack of lies to accomplish it."

I gasped when I heard the district attorney's words, for nothing could be further from the truth. I was about to leap to my feet to say it was not true but Franklin Dale held me back.

"Call Patsy Branson to the stand, Abe Clark said. I went into a kind of shock when Patsy walked into the courtroom I had thought I might never see her again. She looked at me and I thought my heart would burst wide open. No one in that courtroom except Patsy and I knew just how much each of us needed the support of the other at this moment, her eyes said volumes to me but we could not speak to each other.

"State your name and relationship to the accused?" Clark barked at her.

"Patsy Branson. I am Clem Branson's wife."

Did you ever discuss with the accused the possibility of the Branson farm becoming his at the death of his father?"

"Yes. Before we came to live there after Clem got out of the army, we had to decide whether we would come back to Gage County or find work elsewhere."

"So you did discuss taking over the farm at Jed Branson's death?"

"Yes, but not in the way you are suggesting."

"I am suggesting nothing Mrs. Branson. Did you discuss with your husband the intent to murder Jed Branson in order for you both to take over the farm?"

"No"

"Did you co-conspire with the accused to tell a pack of lies, including that Jed Branson had raped you, a devoutly Christian man who had opened his heart and his home to you both?"

"No. It's not true!" Abe Clark turned to the jury,

"This witness has admitted speaking with her husband about taking over the Branson farm when Jed Branson was dead. I say to you this woman conspired with the accused to get their greedy hands on the farm much sooner than Jed Branson's natural death." Turning back to face Patsy he asked, "is it true Mrs Branson that my investigators located you at the Branson farmhouse already changing the house to your own personal wants and doing laundry? Were those garments laundered to remove bloodstains after helping your husband murder your father in law?"

"No of course not."

"Did the accused ever assault his father while at the Branson farm?"

"Yes they had a fight on the day we arrived because his father."

107

"A simple yes will suffice Mrs. Branson."

"No further questions at this time your honor." Franklin Dale wobbled to his feet and faced Patsy.

"Were you raped by Jed Branson and were you running away from the farm after that rape when you met your husband on the road and told him about it?"

"Yes,"

"What happened after that Mrs. Branson?"

"I kept on running. I did not know what else to do. I ran across the fields and hid in some trees until the next morning. I was afraid to go back to the farm but I crept back there to replace my torn clothing making sure that Jed Branson didn't spot me and that's when I discovered blood all over the kitchen and I thought the old man must have killed Clem. I walked all the way into town and that's when I discovered that it was Clem who had killed his father."

"Did you know your husband was going to murder his father?"

"No I did not."

"Why was there a fight on the day of your arrival?"

"Jed Branson. Struck the first blow after Clem told him that now that he and I were married there would have to be some new rules regarding pay and division of duties. I guess the old man expected Clem to continue working for free with me also working alongside him."

"Can you tell the court what happened on the day of the rape?"

Clem had gone into town with a load of beans and I was busy preserving peas. The old man came up behind me and grabbed me. He threw me down on the kitchen floor, tore my clothing then he raped me. When he had finished he got up and I escaped from the house and began running. On the road I met my husband, I told him what had happened and kept right on running. I have not seen Clem until today in this court."

"Thank you Mrs. Branson. No further questions."

I cannot describe the pain I felt for Patsy as she told the court her story, then Abe Clark rose to his feet to cross-examine.

"Mrs. Branson can you tell the court why you did not report the alleged rape to the police or why you did not seek medical attention to corroborate your story?"

"I was too frightened and shocked. It never crossed my mind."

"I suggest to you and to the jury that the rape never happened. Jed Branson was a lifelong churchgoer, pious to a fault as confirmed by his pastor. Such a thing would be completely out of character. I also suggest to the jury that this woman conspired with her husband to murder Jed Branson to obtain his farm and property. Members of the jury there can only be one verdict in this case. The accused has already confessed to the murder of his father. He is a cold-blooded killer ladies and gentlemen, deserving of the full weight of the law. You must find him guilty as charged." Abe Clark went to sit down with a smile on his face I fully expected Franklin Dale to stand and speak on my behalf. To tell the court the truth about my upbringing, about my service to my country and being wounded in that service. But he sat and made no attempt to defend my actions before the jury.

They were only out of the courtroom for five minutes when they came back with a verdict of guilty. The judge sentenced me to twenty-five years in the State Penitentiary with no opportunity for parole. I spent one more night in the local jail and the next morning they transported me in chains to the State Penitentiary in Watson County.

About fifteen newly convicted men were my companions as I rode in a bus with wire mesh covered windows. We were all pretty nervous not really knowing what to expect on our arrival at the state penitentiary. Alongside the bus driver, a guard sat facing us holding a large gauge shotgun. He reminded me of my military boot camp sergeant, big-shouldered heavy set and with a face as hard as granite. I got the uneasy feeling that he would not hesitate for a second pulling the trigger on any miscreant on the bus. The look on his face as though we were vermin brought back memories of my father's looks at me when he was displeased. A shiny chain connected to each of our leg shackles ran between the supports on the bus seats to a heavy ring on the bus floor near the guard's feet.

It took about an hour for our transport to reach the penitentiary. When we did there was no mistaking it. Tall gray concrete walls higher than the roof of the average house topped by tangled barbed wire hid from our view the gigantic blockhouse inside. Our bus driver sounded the horn and the doors pushed by two shotgun toting guards opened wide allow the bus to enter my new home. We proceeded to a wire caged reception area and our connecting chain and shackles were removed. Our personal belongings in labeled large paper sacks were emptied from under the bus and taken away.

The prison head warden began to address us.

"You have all been sentenced by the courts to serve your time of incarceration in this facility. I warn you in

110

advance I run a tight ship. To date no one has escaped from my jurisdiction, to consider it is futile. We have strict rules of conduct, deviate from them and swift harsh punishment will follow. Obey them to the letter and your time served will be much easier. Since we do not know what type of environment you hail from, you will all be deloused before entering the building. You will be assigned a prison number, cell and clothing. Carry on Jackman." The warden said to an officer, and then he turned and went inside.

"Strip," Jackman bellowed. We did as ordered and then a prisoner with a sprayer began to hose us down with foul smelling insecticide. We stood dripping for five minutes or so before being marched in naked to receive our prison garb. An eight digit prison number and cell were assigned to each of us then a guard led me to the third tier of cells, my new home for the next twenty-five years.

I found I had to share my quarters with a man convicted of killing his wife. He pointed to the top bunk,

"Yours," he said curtly. My immediate thought was I would spend my time with a man of few words like my father. I just hoped he wasn't a religious fanatic like him. The truth is I would have preferred the top bunk anyway, there was much more space between the mattress and the ceiling.

"I'm Clem Branson," I said by way of introduction.

"Hank Battagliola," my cellmate replied offering me his hand. He had a voice so he was not like my father after all. I discovered later that his gruff greeting was a territorial defense strategy common throughout the prison. Neither was Hank a religious nut. Once we understood each other we became friends. He had received a good education and was knowledgeable in a great many things, he filled me in on the prison dos and don'ts and informed me on a number of educational services offered within the prison. It seemed odd, but in the following weeks we did not speak about the acts that had brought us to this place.

I missed Patsy terribly, especially at nights lying on my bunk trying to ignore the many noises of the cellblock. Some nights were worse than others and from time to time I wept quietly for her, wishing I could be next to her and worrying about where she was and how she was getting along. If Hank heard me weeping he never said anything for we had developed a mutual understanding of each other's feelings.

I had been in the penitentiary for about six weeks when the guard informed me I had a visitor.

"Who is it?" I inquired.

"They don't tell me who it is Branson, just to come and get you." He answered in a surly voice. He led me to the visitor's room. It reminded me of the chicken coop back on the farm. They sat me down in front of some heavy mesh and then, Patsy walked in at the other side. Suddenly I felt overcome with joy at seeing her; I experienced surprise and an utter feeling of helplessness since I could not even hold her hand. Tears came and rolled down my cheeks. I looked at Patsy and saw she too wept at seeing me.

"Are you all right Clem?" she asked

"Yes Patsy my love, I'm all right but I miss you terribly." I drew in a deep breath and regained control of my emotions. "Patsy. I have been thinking about what I am about to say and because I love you so deeply I must say it. I wish to set you free, Patsy. I am locked in here for twenty-five years and I will not ask you to wait for me. I want you to go and make a new life for yourself, marry again if you want, I will not contest a divorce it that is what you need. But please go out and start afresh, forget about me. In all conscience I would not have it any other way." Patsy wept at hearing my words and through her tears I knew she wanted to tell me something, but she stood up blew me a goodbye kiss and left the visitors room.

I had sealed my own fate. The one person in the entire world that I loved I had set free and I wished her well. As for me she would be the only person I would ever love but there was no turning back. I would remember her in my mind and when I got out of here as a middle aged man I would remember her through the carving I had made of her that lay in the bag of my possessions.

In my second year of incarceration I received another visitor. Mr. Galbraithe was a lawyer for Gage County.

"Mr. Branson. The county engaged me to handle the Branson family affairs after your conviction. After non-payment of taxes the Branson farm and the house and equipment were auctioned off to the highest bidder. After auctioneer fees, taxes, transfer fees, and legal fees I regret to say that most of the proceeds have been swallowed up. There is a balance of just five hundred and forty five dollars which has been deposited in your name in the Gage County Mercantile Bank. I need you to sign some documents and I will give you a bank passbook."

I had no regrets about losing the farm it had nothing

but bad memories for me, so I agreed to sign without a fuss. I took advantage of all the educational programs the penitentiary offered. Not only did I learn the things I should have learned in school had I been able to attend, but also it helped take my mind off Patsy at least during daylight hours.

I had been inside thirty-six months when out of the blue I received instructions to report to the warden's office. To say the least I felt highly nervous at this turn of events it could mean almost anything, a transfer perhaps, an infraction of a rule I might be unaware of and the punishment for it.

"Sit down Branson," the warden said in a calm friendly sounding voice. "You have been with us for thirty-six months Branson. You have been a model prisoner and I see by your records you are availing yourself of our educational programs. To say the least I am most pleased with your conduct and progress. I have here in your file a letter written by Sheriff Coltrane of the Gage County police. In fact the letter has been here since you arrived. Sheriff Coltrane asks me in his letter to take into consideration that you are basically a good citizen, that you had a rough upbringing and that you were fully cooperative with the police in the investigation and also that you had never tried to dodge your responsibility. He also says you had recently come home from Korea as a wounded veteran and further that your crime in his opinion was completely understandable in the circumstances.

Sheriff Coltrane asks me to try to give you special consideration while in my custody but I am sure Branson that you realize I could not immediately grant special privileges to a new inmate or I might end up with a riot on my hands. You have earned the respect of the other prisoners and at this point if I were to offer special privileges they would understand that you have earned them. In my entire career I have never had such a letter from a law enforcement officer and I must tell you Branson it carries a lot of weight. Tell me Branson what can the penitentiary do to make your stay with us more bearable?"

I did not know what to say. The warden's words came as a complete surprise. I think I must have sat for a full minute with my mouth wide open. When I finally began to think I said,

"I would like to take up my carving again."

"Carving?"

"Yes sir I would like to start carving again. I used to be very good at it. In fact my carving tools are in my bag of personal effects."

"What kind of carving Branson. Stone, marble, wood?"

"I work in wood sir."

"Very well, Branson. I will arrange for you to use a corner of the carpentry shop but as a security the tools will have to be kept there under lock and key when you are not working."

"Then I will carve a dove for you warden, it is the symbol of freedom."

"I know Branson, I know."

So began yet another phase of my life. When not attending my educational classes I worked at my carving in a corner of the carpentry shop I had other tools at my disposal to make the work easier, I could cut out the

115

rough outline of my projects using a band saw and I had electric drills and sanders. To show my appreciation to the warden and also to showcase my skills I produced a dove with a wingspan of two feet. Carved to the minutest detail with every feather looking like a real feather. With the paint supplies in the cupboards I gave the dove gray eyes ringed with black and red legs with ivory claws, his body pure white with tinges of gray for shadow.

"It is magnificent Branson!" The warden exclaimed when I presented it to him. It will hang here in my office. Can you carve other things beside birds?

"Yes sir. I believe I can carve anything, given the time and the right materials to work with." The warden's high praise boosted my ego. My feelings of self worth began to flow through my veins like a spring freshet. I felt pride like in the moment when I presented Patsy with the carving of her likeness. A lump came to my throat as I thought of her for she would have been so proud of my achievement.

"Then come with me, Branson. Have I got a job for you." The warden led me through the penitentiary hallways to the chapel. He pointed to a simple wooden cross hanging on the wall above a plain wood altar.

"What can you do with that, Branson?"

"I can make it beautiful, warden. With a likeness of Christ fastened up upon it with nails, but I would make the nails from wood and when it is completed I could carve the scene of the last supper onto the altar."

"Tell me what you need; Branson and you can get started when you are ready."

"I will need a twelve by twelve block of wood six feet long for the body of Christ and a piece of six by six for the arms also about six feet long and I will carve it in three pieces and put them together when it is time to mount it upon the cross."

"I will get them delivered as soon as possible."

This project was a lifesaver for me. No longer had I to spend many hours lying on my bunk staring at the concrete ceiling above me. Now I could spend my time being productive and using my mother's gift to create a work of art. Each time I picked up the carving kit I thought of her and sometimes I wondered if she could look down from the heavens and see what I was doing. If she could, I knew she would be very proud of her son. It took seven months of diligent work to complete the Christ figure. Big square pegs carved to look like nails with large heads fastened the finished work to the original plain cross.

The warden was ecstatic and the prison chaplain dedicated the work on the symbolic day of Good Friday. I felt very proud when many of the inmates congratulated me on the magnificence of the work. The accolades gave me the impetus to begin immediately on the altar. Rather than work on the original wood I decided I would carve three large slabs to cover the front and one specially cut slab for the top. It took me a year to complete but since it had been a labor of love, I hardly noticed how quickly the time had passed. Over the next five years I carved the twelve apostles mounting them on pedestals around the perimeter of the chapel.

During this time I had received sufficient education to enter college were I free to do so. One day during my ninth year of incarceration the State Governor came to visit the penitentiary. The warden proudly showed the

Governor the chapel and he asked to see me.

"You have done a magnificent job Mr. Branson, your carvings are exquisite. The warden tells me you are a model prisoner you obey the rules, are never insolent and have been willing to learn during your time here. I congratulate you Mr. Branson." I nodded an appreciation of his words.

The governor must have talked to the press about what he had seen in the State Pen for almost overnight the press wanted to photograph the interior of the chapel and speak with me. Of course I had to let the warden speak on my behalf, after all I was a prison inmate a convicted murderer.

I had begun work carving bible scenes on the chapel's entry doors when I got the call to visit the warden's office

"Branson," he said, "The Governor was greatly impressed with your work here, your attitude and willingness to learn. Accordingly he has begun to look into your case to see if a Governor's pardon is in order. It will certainly get my support if it comes to that. I tell you this Branson not to get your hopes up but simply to inform you what is going on behind the scenes."

The news unnerved me. I could not concentrate on the carving; the tools seemed extra heavy I could swear that my mother held the same chisels I did, giving me her silent support like she had when I was still a child. The time that had passed so quickly when the work totally engrossed me, now dragged interminably since hearing the warden's news of a possible pardon. As always the wheels of officialdom turn slowly and after six months I had given up on the idea I would be freed before my time. In fact the thought of early freedom scared me a little, what could I do out there. I thought of following my early dreams of becoming a long haul truck driver burning up the roads of America. But who would hire a felon, especially one convicted of murder. I had a feeling that my good behaviour in here would cut no ice out in the real world. Going back to the army was not an option; they wouldn't want a gimpy-legged man they had already rejected. I might be able to get a dead end job as a dishwasher or I suppose I could go back to bean farming working for someone else, but it was the last thing I wanted to do. However at this stage getting work out outside the penitentiary didn't matter a hill of beans. After all this time I figured the pardon issue had died a quiet death. I thought back to the act that had put me here. I saw my father's face before me staring phantom like and I remembered how I never saw him smile.

CHAPTER SIX.

Patsy Branson worked at the kitchen sink shelling peas picked from the garden that morning. Deftly using finger and thumb she shelled and put the peas directly into mason jars ready for preserving. The empty pods she put into the sink to be fed to the pig later in the day. The heat from the woodstove added to the warmth of the day. Knowing she would be working in elevated temperatures she had opted to wear a thin cotton dress and work without her bra, assuming her father-in-law would be out working the fields.

Humming a tune as she worked, Patsy did not hear Jed Branson step into the kitchen. The first thing she noticed that things were going awry was the foul smell of chewing tobacco juice from close by. Turning swiftly, Jed Branson's face leered at her from much too close for comfort. Wet tobacco juice dripped from his lower lip and his eyes had the look of evil in them. Hatless, his stringy and greasy hair fell over his ears and forehead. Patsy moved to get away from him; he made her feel very uncomfortable. He stepped in front of her as she moved sideways and blocked her. Darting hands with blackened fingernails grabbed the front of her dress. The top several buttons tore off exposing her breasts to him. The hands darted again and cupped each breast.

"Stop it!" Patsy shrieked. But Jed Branson paid her no mind. Patsy squirmed trying to turn and get away from him. More buttons succumbed to his tugging. Using his superior strength he forced her to the floor amid the peas spilled in the scuffle. Holding her down with one arm he wrenched at her panties. They tore leaving her exposed. He knelt on her stomach and pulled his overall straps from his shoulders. Patsy struggled valiantly knowing Jed Branson was about to rape her but she was no match for the wiry attacker. Jed shoved his overalls down past his buttocks, forced her legs apart and proceeded to violate her. When he had completed his evil act, he stood and looked at her as though she were less than dirt.

Patsy clambered to her feet, wrapping the remains of her dress around her she ran from the house. With no real idea of where she was bound clutching her dress to her body, she ran through the farm gates out onto the road. Her mind a tangle of hurt, horror, disgust and an intense sense of her entire being having been violated in a most crude act of violence, out of habit she ran towards the town. Right now she needed the comfort and support of her husband but he had left her behind. Suddenly anger toward him for leaving her behind added itself to the emotional mix running through her brain. Strength came from deep within her. Running as she had never run before her legs propelled her forward effortlessly. Patsy felt that running was the only way for her to recover from the tangle of fears and emotions controlling her. She had no idea how long she had been running when in the distance she saw the farm truck approaching. It stopped as it neared her. Clem called to her from the cab and she answered,

"Your father raped me!" She kept on running. In her state of mental turmoil it did not occur to her that Clem might be able to comfort her. Right now at this moment, nothing could ease her mind so she continued to run. Patsy saw from the corner of her eye that Clem ran after her, but he soon gave up went back to the truck and that was the last she saw of him. Perhaps it was a survival instinct she didn't really know, Patsy suddenly leapt the roadside ditch and ran headlong across a harvested bean field toward a group of trees about a half mile from the road. Her disturbed mind told her she could shelter and be safe there. Out of sight of the road in a small hollow amid the trees the exertion of her run quickly revealed itself and she collapsed to her knees gasping for breath. When her breathing slowed the tears started. Patsy gathered her tattered dress around her and lay in the fetal position weeping until darkness covered the land.

At some point in the middle of the night she began to shiver with the cold and by the time the sun had risen, her thinking had righted itself. She decided she would go back to the farm to find Clem and insist that they leave that very day. No longer would she live on the same property as the evil Jed Branson. With her throat dry and her face tear stained, Patsy walked back the way she had come. She hesitated at the farm gate, the last thing she wanted was to step back on the farm and find she was once again alone with Jed Branson. No smoke curled out of the chimney and the chickens wandered around the yard waiting to be fed. The truck sat in the barn so she deduced they must be out working the fields.

Patsy went to the barn where she knew several raincoats hung; she put one on to cover her torn dress. Then she crept quietly to the house and listened for sounds of human activity. There were none. Patsy opened the door. The sight that met her eyes appalled her. The kitchen floor blackened by dried blood, bloodied footprints coming out to the porch, blood smeared handprints were on the side of the stove. The peas she had been shelling stood out green in the dried blood looking like macabre measles spots.

It was obvious someone had been murdered here. Had the old man killed Clem? According to Clem the old man had always hated him for reasons he did not know. Where had he taken the body? Had the old man slipped over the edge of sanity and gone completely mad? Was he hiding somewhere on the farm waiting for her to come back and murder her too? A chill ran through Patsy's body at the thought. She went to the utensils drawer and took out the pig-killing knife then opened the back bedroom door. He wasn't there nor was he in the bathroom or anywhere in the house. Feeling a little safer, Patsy washed and dressed while trying to avoid stepping in the blood on the floor.

Now she had to think of the immediate future. If Clem had been murdered she would have to make a new life for herself. She would go back to San Francisco, and then reality struck. She had no money. Then she remembered the tin the old man had taken a wad of bills out of for her and Clem to go shopping on the second morning they were here. Stepping carefully she retrieved the tin from the shelf, it contained only two dollars. It would not buy her a good meal, let alone the train fare out to the West Coast. Patsy thought about packing her belongings and leaving, but she realized she could not walk all that way carrying a heavy bag. She put two sets of underwear and a change of dress in a paper bag.

At that moment she heard a movement in the kitchen. She froze. Filled with fear that Jed Branson had come back to finish her off. Patsy picked up the pig-killing knife, gripping the handle tightly so it would not slip should she have to defend herself. Patsy stepped lightly into the kitchen with her heart beating wildly. She was fully ready to fight for her life if need be, but her fear was short lived, a hungry chicken had wandered in through the open door and busily pecked at the spilled peas on the floor. Regaining her composure she took a deep breath and left the house.

On the way to the road she noticed the damaged gatepost and wondered how it had happened. Very little traffic traveled the road to town mainly it would be farmers either getting supplies or delivering beans to the co-op. Consequently, Patsy walked the full eight miles into town without being able to catch a ride. The long walk gave her ample time to think about how much she loved him and how she would miss Clem being in her life. Also plenty of time to worry how she would manage to get by with no money until she could find a job that paid enough to allow her to live and save the train fare to San Francisco.

Walking into town, she passed a variety store. Patsy could not help but see the words on the newspaper billboard.

**Tragedy hits Branson farm on County Road. # 4
Local farm boy admits to killing his father.**

Patsy's heart stopped when she realized that Clem had not died. It took only a microsecond for her to figure that Clem had gone to the house after meeting her on the road and had killed his father in anger and revenge for raping her. She also understood that Clem being an honest and moral man would have turned himself in to the authorities. Now a whole new series of emotions invaded her mind. She felt relief that the love of her life had not died. Fear of what would become of him and an odd sense of gratitude that Clem loved her so much he had killed a man for violating her. Patsy knew she must go to him knowing him well enough that he would be worrying about her, especially since she had run away from him on the road in her state of panic.

Her feet hurt from the long walk into town but she asked the way to the Sheriff's office and inquired.

"I have come to see my husband Clem Branson."

"Only lawyers representing the accused are allowed to visit prisoners in the pretrial cells." The desk clerk told her coldly. "A trial date has been set and you can come to the courtroom and see him there. If he is convicted, you will have to visit him at the State Penitentiary." Patsy left feeling utterly dejected. She needed to tell Clem that she loved him and she needed to hear it from him. She had no money and nowhere to go and now she was hungry and tired, no longer could she lean on Clem for any kind of support.

Her first thought for shelter was the railroad station. In San Francisco many people spent the night in the stations, perhaps she could find somewhere safe and warm in the station here. On sore feet she made her way there, only to find it closed until seven in the morning. After exhausting many ideas she recalled Clem speaking of the pastor in the church he and his father frequented. Perhaps he might be able to aid her. She found the church and the big red brick house on the lot next to it and rapped on the front door.

"Please father I need help? Patsy said when the door opened.

"I am not Catholic young lady. This is a Baptist church. Perhaps you are looking for the parish of St Michael; the church is over on Walnut Street."

"No sir. This is the church my husband, Clem Branson used to come to before he went with the army to Korea. Something terrible has happened. I have no money and nowhere to spend the night. I got the feeling from Clem that you might be the one to help me?"

"You had best step inside young lady and tell me what your problem is, have you had a fight with your husband?"

"No sir. It's much worse than that." Patsy followed him into his office where he motioned her to sit.

"It's hard for me to say sir. When my husband came to town yesterday with a load of beans his father, Jed Branson came into the farm kitchen threw me down and raped me."

"Jed Branson! It does not sound like the Jed Branson I know. Are you sure?"

"Yes sir. I ran from the farm and met my husband on the way back from town in the truck. I can't explain now why, but I just yelled at him that his father had raped

126

me. I kept on running then I hid among some trees until this morning. I walked back to the farm to find my husband but he was not there, the house was covered in blood and I knew someone had been murdered in the house although there was no body. I thought Jed Branson had killed Clem and removed his corpse, for it is true he seemed to hate his son. I dared not stay at the house in case the old man intended to murder me too. I have no money and have walked all the way here. On the billboard of the variety store I saw the latest news, it said that my husband had killed his father and confessed to the Sheriff's Department. I have been there but they will not allow me to see him." Having got the story out, Patsy began to cry.

"Jed Branson is one of the most faithful and devout members of my congregation I must admit I find your story hard to believe young lady. Are you sure you are not making this up?"

"No it's all true," Patsy sobbed. The pastor picked up his phone and dialed. Patsy could tell he spoke with the Sheriff's Department.

"Well you are right. Jed Branson is dead and they are holding your husband for trial surely there is some money in the house and a bed you can sleep in there?"

"I found only two dollars and I cannot sleep there, for there is blood everywhere even on the stove."

We have a small room in the church we use for destitute people. I will allow you to use it for tonight we are not running a hotel you should go back to the family home tomorrow and clean the place up so you can live in it. I'm sure that's what your husband would expect you to do under the circumstances. Surely you Branson's have credit at the bean co-op general store; you should be able to manage. Follow me I will take you to the church. Just one night mind you!"

Patsy had a distinct feeling that the pastor felt he was dealing with a degenerate sinner deserving of contempt, but his calling prevented him from sending her to the streets. The tiny room had two cots and a hotplate sitting on a chest of six drawers. In an even smaller adjoining room sat a bathtub, sink and flush toilet. Patsy began to fill the bath while checking the drawers; she found a kettle, saucepan, some coffee and several cans of local baked beans.

The hot water and soap removed the surface dirt from her skin, but it could not rid it of the memory of being raped by Jed Branson. No matter how much she scrubbed it the sense of his foulness lingered. The temple of her body she had given to Clem as his bride had been brutally defiled and no scrubbing, soap, or water could change that. When she had dried off, Patsy heated and ate a can of beans then exhausted, slipped into one of the cots.

It would be the loneliest night of her life. A strange bed, in a strange room in an even stranger building, her husband across town in a prison cell charged with murder and in a town where she knew no one that she could call a friend. Patsy awakened from a troubled sleep as the sun reached deep into the church basement through the high window. While the kettle boiled to make coffee, she made up the bed and tidied the room.

Patsy had decided to take the pastor's advice and go back to the farm. There remained no longer any real danger and it would give her time to make permanent plans. She washed the cup and saucepan, replaced them in the drawers and left the way she had entered last night. About a mile out of the town she heard a vehicle coming up behind her so she held out her arm with her thumb upturned to ask for a ride. The farm truck stopped Patsy climbed in and the driver asked,

"Where are you headed?"

"I'm going to the Branson farm," Patsy replied.

"Are you Jed Branson's boy's wife?"

"Yes I'm Patsy Branson."

"Did you know the boy murdered old Jed the day before yesterday?" Patsy nodded. "What happened to make the boy kill his father?"

"The old man raped me and I guess Clem killed him on account of it. I haven't seen him since. He is in jail at the Sheriff's Office and they won't let me see him."

'Try not to worry too much young lady," the driver said putting his hand on her leg. Patsy was immediately repulsed, plainly the man was attempting to take advantage of her vulnerability.

"Let me out! Stop the truck! She screamed.

"There's no need for you to get so uppity, you can't blame a man for trying. Calm down. I'll drop you off at the Branson farm gate." They rode the rest of the way in silence and when the vehicle stopped, Patsy stepped out and slammed the door without a word of thanks then strode through the farm gate. The sound of human feet started the starving pig squealing to be fed and a flock of hungry chickens ran toward her eagerly expecting her to be carrying a pail of feed. The animals were blameless in the situation so she saw to their needs before going to the house to begin cleaning up Jed Branson's spilled blood. The act of feeding the stock made her realize that they could be sold for cash to cover her train fare to San Francisco if Clem was convicted and sent to the state prison.

Patsy had mixed emotions cleaning the kitchen, disgust at what had to be done and an odd feeling of gratitude to Clem for avenging her. She was busy washing the cleaning cloths along with some personal laundry when investigators from the district attorneys office called and asked to examine the house; they poked around for a while then left. For a week Patsy took care of the house and farm animals, but by then kitchen supplies were running low. She had never driven before having no driver's license. She decided to try and start the truck and take it into town. She found it much too daunting for the walk both ways carrying groceries on the way back. Having watched Clem do it she managed to get the engine running and with much gear grinding managed to back it out of the barn, get it into forward gear then off she went.

At the bean co-op general store she ordered the things she needed and told the clerk to

"Put it on the Branson account."

"I'm sorry Ma'am I can't do that. Mr. Branson is dead and his son is in pre-trial custody charged with his murder. We cannot extend any further credit to the Branson account until the balance is paid up to date. We need to have some proof that the Branson farm will continue to produce beans for the co-op. The fact is Ma'am we will be sending out a truck to empty the Branson bean silo's to be sure we are paid what the farm already owes us."

"If there is sufficient in the silo's to clear off the account will I be able to charge groceries then?"

"I would think not Ma'am. Firstly there is no account in either yours or your husband's names. Secondly there is the matter of the grower's contract; with the death of Jed Branson the contract is null and void. We will be happy to supply you with groceries but on a cash basis only."

"But I have no cash and I must have some supplies."

"I'm sorry Ma'am no cash, no supplies." Patsy walked out of the co-op furious that the clerk had no compassion for her plight. She started the truck and started back to the farm. Flashing red lights and a wailing siren as she left the town limits brought her to a halt.

"You are driving that truck in second gear with the engine racing Miss," the deputy said.

"Can I see your drivers licence?"

Still angry Patsy answered in a sharp voice,

"I have no damn drivers licence, this is an emergency or I wouldn't be driving this thing."

"Show me the registration papers?"

"What are they and where would I find them?" The deputy stared at her.

"Step out of the truck Ma'am. Now!" Patsy complied while the deputy rummaged through the glove box and found the papers. "This is Jed Branson's truck. What are you doing with it, have you stolen it?"

"Of course not I'm Patsy Branson. Jed Branson's daughter in law."

"Wife of the fellow that murdered him?"

"Yes."

"Mrs. Branson. It is against the law in this state to

drive without a license and it is against the law to drive a motor vehicle without the express permission of the registered owner. I'm sorry but I cannot permit you to continue driving it. The vehicle will be towed to the impound lot and held until the impound fees are paid. I am giving you a citation for driving without the proper permit. You may pay the fine at the courthouse." The deputy took the keys and sat in his car and spoke to someone on his radio.

Patsy started walking toward the farm. She felt that the whole town had turned against her and it was all as a result of being raped by Clem's father. She had the feeling the townsfolk knowing Jed Branson to be a regular church attendee and who knew nothing of the rape, probably believed Clem to be a criminal type and she as his wife shared the branding.

Patsy arrived at the farm weary, angry and footsore. Two large trucks were emptying the bean silos and a note pinned to the house door said that the county animal control officers had removed the farm livestock in accordance with bylaw 49650L, on account of them having been deemed abandoned. Not only would there be no more eggs, but the opportunity to sell the livestock for travel money had been taken from her. Until the day of Clem's trial, Patsy sustained herself on produce from the garden, loose beans from the silo floor and the final salt cured ham hanging in the larder. A deputy delivered a subpoena to the farm, on the day of the trial she had to be up early to walk into town. The loneliness was almost unbearable; Jed Branson's surly attitude had ensured that neighbouring farmers stayed clear of the Branson place. No one came to offer any help and the worst part, was the appalling emptiness in her heart without Clem to comfort her. A new concern invaded Patsy's dejected self, her monthly indisposition was overdue and she put it down to diet or stress but the knowledge nagged at her. She and Clem had always used contraceptives and the fear that Jed Branson had impregnated her during the rape grew with each passing day.

On the long walk to the courthouse she had to stop to vomit. In her mind it meant her worst fear had come to fruition. She carried Jed Branson's child. It would be half brother to her husband, a man going on trial this very day for murdering the child's father. Patsy arrived at the courthouse exhausted and sick in mind and spirit. She would likely be testifying against her husband and she would not be able to speak with him privately and tell him the awful news.

When the court convicted Clem sentencing him the State Penitentiary, Patsy learned that it would be six weeks before she could visit him there. She felt that she could not just leave for San Francisco without telling Clem of her situation face to face. Getting a job in town was completely out of the question for she could not possibly walk the almost sixteen miles round trip and work each day, so she stayed on at the Branson farm with scarcely any variety in her diet.

Patsy hitchhiked all the way to the penitentiary in Watson County and waited to see Clem. After initial greetings and affirmations of love for each other, Clem without giving her a chance to tell him of her problems, told her he wanted to set her free and she should look to making a new life for herself and telling her to get a divorce if she needed one. For Patsy his words were the last straw, she left the prison and immediately began hitchhiking out to California. It took her four hungry and tired days to reach San Francisco and the apartment of her friend Margery.

A boy child came into the world, Jed Branson's child. Patsy feared looking at the baby's face at his birth in case it looked rat like and evil. All through the pregnancy she had considered giving the child up at birth for adoption. The thought of constantly looking into the face of a young version of Jed Branson was more than she could bear to think about.

It had been a difficult time the last nine months. Clem's words of dismissal at the penitentiary, without giving her a chance to tell him of the difficulty she faced. Being pregnant as a result of the rape and the financial trials she faced. Patsy still loved him desperately and missed him even more. They were pointless emotions given the circumstances of him being locked away for such a longtime. Patsy realized she would be close to forty-five years old when the authorities let Clem go. There had been the difficulty of adjusting to living with and accepting charity from her friend, Margery until she found work and they found a larger place to accommodate both of them. Margery had been more than charitable but she had formed a style of living much different than Pasty's. While they never openly argued there was an underlying sense of friction between them. It took considerable time before Patsy could pay her share of the apartment rent and re-stock her wardrobe. Margery had come from a middle-income family while Patsy had grown up poor and there remained between them a different philosophy about money that had not been apparent when they were just friends. The telephone company graciously re-employed her as a switchboard operator so having a sit down job; Patsy had been able to continue working until her labor pains started.

"You have a fine healthy baby boy, Mrs. Branson," the delivery room nurse said cheerfully as Patsy recovered from the final effort of giving birth. In the last few minutes of acute agony she wished the child would be born dead relieving her of Jed Branson's curse upon her life. The nurse's cheerful words let loose a plethora of emotions. She needed Clem now more than anything, she needed his strength, his simple way of making her feel right and she needed to feel his gentle touch. The child she had wished had died, lived and according to the nurse in robust health. If she did not give up the child for adoption he would be a major obstacle in rebuilding her life also possibly a continuation of Jed Branson's cruelty through him.

The nurse's words brought on a pitiful wail of distress from Patsy, tears began to gush and deep-heaving sobs racked her already fragile body.

"You must not cry like this Mrs. Branson you may harm yourself. I will bring your baby to you it will help calm you." In a few moments, Patsy felt a small bundle being slipped into her arms. "What will you call him Mrs. Branson?" Patsy did not reply. Naming the child and a christening ceremony were the furthest thing from her mind. She dared not open her eyes to see the child, in case her worst fears were realized. "Open your eyes and see your beautiful child for the first time Mrs. Branson," the nurse urged.

Reluctantly opening one eye, Patsy saw not the face

of, Jed Branson but of a miniature Clem looking up expectantly at her. She lowered her head and kissed the child's forehead. Instantly, she knew she could not give the child up for adoption. He was part of her, no matter the circumstances of his conception.

Life made a sudden and dramatic change; the care of her baby took priority over everything. With buying the necessary baby items and paying her share of household expenses her meagre savings dwindled quickly. All too soon she had to put baby John Branson into daycare while she returned to her job at the phone company. Often she toyed with the idea of writing a note to Clem, but each time she thought better of it. It really would serve no purpose other than to upset him; finding out his father had impregnated her and produced a son. But she longed for some kind of contact with him; even a short note would help her to carry on.

Patsy spurned attempts by other men to step into her husband's shoes. The love she and Clem had shared was irreplaceable; she desired no man's touch but his. One day Margery announced that she had accepted a proposal of marriage and would soon be leaving with her new husband to live in San Diego. Patsy and young John now two years old and a regular bundle of mischief, moved into a basement suite in a house just off Sutter St. The house was close to the bus route, the day care and the primary school where John Branson began lessons at age five. He approached his tenth birthday when once again life for Patsy Branson took another dramatic turn.

Reading the newspaper in the telephone company lunchroom, Patsy's gaze became riveted on a short article on page seven.

State Governor to Pardon Murderer.
Governor George Patterson has offered a
complete pardon to Clement Branson.
A convicted murderer in recognition
of his exemplary behaviour and his
magnificent contribution of carvings
to the penitentiary chapel. It is expected
The pardon will take effect on the tenth
anniversary of his incarceration.

Patsy stared at the article open mouthed. She read it over and over trying to get it to sink in that Clem would soon be free. She tore the page out of the paper and put it in her purse. When young John had been put to bed that night she agonized over what she would do. It had been ten years, but she wanted Clem just as much as she did when they were newlyweds. Her first instinct was to write and tell Clem she was here in San Francisco and for him to hurry to her. But he knew nothing of the child and John knew nothing of his real father, or indeed of her husband Clem. She had shielded him from the truth, wishing to spare him the shame of having his mother's husband in prison for murder and to hide her own feelings of shame having been raped and he being the result of it.

Patsy wished desperately that she had told John a few simple facts when he was much younger; it would have made today's decision so much easier. Chances are he would have filed the information away in his mind and not dwell on it. Now it would probably be a big deal knowing his whole life had been based on withheld truths.

What of Clem? It had been ten years with no contact between them. There was a possibility he had developed a lifestyle that didn't include her. Things happened in prisons she had heard about it. Could it be that Clem might now prefer the company of men? On the other hand he may long to be with her. But at this point he would have no idea if she were alive or dead or where she might be living. How after all this time would he react to the truth about John? Would he summarily reject him, cautiously accept him, or love him unconditionally as she did. Would Clem want to return to the Branson Bean farm and begin to work the land and grow beans again? Patsy knew in her heart that if was what Clem intended to do, she would never return to the accursed farm with him.

There were so many reasons to write to Clem and equally as many reasons not to. She sat pen in hand with paper before her but wrote not a single word until the small hours of the morning. Then she wrote, *my darling Clem* but could write no more. Tears filled her eyes so she went to bed needing more time to think. The short time between going to bed and waking to face the next day she dreamed of a wondrous reunion with Clem but she dreamed also of him going on a rampage learning about John and utterly rejecting him.

All the next day she thought about her problem and made the decision she would write to Clem in the penitentiary, to simply say she had learned of his impending release and give him her San Francisco address. It would then be his decision if he wanted to reconnect. After dinner while John read a book she restarted the letter.

*My dear Clem, I read in the newspaper that the State Governor
Planned to pardon you on the tenth anniversary of your imprisonment.
I have made a new life for myself as you told me to when I visited you.
I have not divorced you, or remarried. Obviously I have no idea what
your future Plans are, or if they include me. Should you wish to see?
me again I am living at 1320 East Forty Second Avenue in San Francisco.
Yours Patsy Branson.*

Patsy addressed and placed a stamp on the envelope
and the next morning on the way to work she paused by
a mailbox. The letter and her uncertain future slipped
into the mailbox. It was done.

CHAPTER SEVEN

Upon returning to my cell after working on carving another panel on the Penitentiary chapel doors I found a letter lying on my bunk. Being an unusual event I turned it over and over in my hands, saw the San Francisco postmark and wondered who on earth in San Francisco would be writing to me. I threw it back on the bunk washed my hands and face then lay down to open and read it. It took mere seconds for me to realize it was from Patsy. After all these years she had written to me. All the years of my quiet desperation, of wanting and needing her, she had written to me. I reached for the small carving I had made for her so long ago it had hung on a nail and I handled it whenever I thought of her. Other prisoners had photographs of their loved ones; all I had was the carving to keep her memory alive. With ten years of my running my hands over it, the carving had developed a dark smooth patina

I clutched it to my breast and let out a bellow of utter joy. The noise from the usually quiet me scared the daylight out of my cellmate in the bunk below.

"What the Hell is the matter, Clem? Are you in pain should I call for the guard?"

"No Hank. I have just received a letter from my wife she has heard about my upcoming release and has written giving me her address in San Francisco."

"San Francisco in sunny California? Will you be going there to find her Clem?"

"I sure will. That's where we met when I came back from Korea."

"Is it true that there are palm trees and that it hardly ever rains?"

"Yes there are palm trees Hank, but it does rain from time to time also they do get a lot of fog rolling in from the ocean and then it can be quite cool."

I tried to cut short the conversation with Hank; I had a lot to think about. I wondered how the very first moments of our initial meeting would go. Would she come to me with open arms welcoming me the way I remembered from ten years earlier? Would she want to make love before we told each other how the last ten years had affected us? Could it be that the missing years had changed Patsy? Her letter did not say she had not found love elsewhere, it read only that she had not remarried. Neither did her letter say that she wanted me to come to San Francisco. It said only that she lived there now.

My initial ecstasy upon opening the letter began to fade. Perhaps Patsy had become involved with another man. If she had, I could place no blame on her because it was I who told her to make a new life and forget about me. Yet she had written to tell me her address. Why? The way things had turned out with my imminent pardon, I deeply regretted sending Patsy away the way I had at the time she came to visit me. But it was done. At the time I thought I would be doing her a huge favor freeing her from the bonds of our marriage, but I could not turn back the clock and change things.

It saddened me terribly, for I realized I could set no real stock on picking up with Patsy where we had left off. I decided I should write to Patsy to let her know I still loved her desperately and how I wanted to come to California and be with her. There was two weeks more to go before they finally send me free out of the front gate, there should be plenty of time for my letter to reach her and get her response. I read the letter again and wondered what exactly Patsy meant by her words, "what your future plans are and if they include me." In those few words I had a feeling she asked me diplomatically to come to San Francisco and start anew without actually saying it. But how could I be sure it was what she meant? Perhaps her writing did not clearly state what she wanted to say.

I borrowed a pen and a few sheets of lined paper from Hank and began to write.

Dear Patsy, I received your most welcome letter today.
It is true; I am to be released with full pardon in two weeks
time. Of course I wish to see you Patsy. Not a day or night
in this place has gone by without my thinking of you. I really
don't know what changes have taken place in your life during
the last ten years. Perhaps you have found another man to love.
If you have, I bear the responsibility for telling you to forget
about me and get on with your life. Yes I will come to
San Francisco soon after they let me out, but frankly I do not

know what to expect when I arrive. Will I be coming for a visit?
Or do you want me back?
Yours always, Clem Branson.

After the prison censor board had cleared my letter it went into the mail and I waited on tenterhooks for her reply. By my final full day here it had not yet arrived. I could only assume that Patsy had not wished to respond to my query. I would be leaving in the morning on the prison bus for Gage County. They brought me my army uniform to wear; the clothes I had worn when I was first arrested. They fed me a special breakfast and the warden came to shake hands and wish me well. He handed me a manila envelope,

"Here are your official pardon papers Clem. You have been a model prisoner and you have gained the respect of all my men. Good luck out there. Oh! By the way, this arrived in the morning mail for you."

"Thank You Sir," I said grasping the envelope then I marched out of the blockhouse and onto the bus. Feverishly I opened the letter,

Dear Clem, Yes I do want you to be apart of my life again.
There has been no other man in my life since you went away.
But there are issues that have to be dealt with when you get
here. I have never stopped loving you; Clem and I hope the gap
between us is not too wide to be healed again.
Hurry to me. Patsy.

I let go a wild hoop and holler. I think the guard on the bus put my outburst down to exuberance at my sudden freedom. After an hour's drive the town's bean elevator came in sight and the bus dropped me off at the Sheriff's Office. I walked inside and asked for Sheriff Coltrane for I wanted to thank him for helping me.

"Where have you been soldier? Sheriff Coltrane retired two years back. Can I help?"

"No thanks," I replied "I just wanted to say thank you to him."

With my bank passbook in my pocket I made my way to the bank and walked inside. I approached a teller gave her my passbook telling her I wished to withdraw the cash and close the account. She looked at my passbook then checked in her files. The woman in a brown tweed suit and with her hair cut short, reminded me of a girl that had attended school in Mrs. Bartoski's house at the time I did.

"Just a moment sir," she said then went into the manager' office. She returned with a portly and pale looking man in his fifties wearing a striped suit with a plain red tie.

"Young Clem Branson! We heard you were getting out. My teller says you wish to close your account and take out the cash Mr. Branson. Unfortunately there is a discrepancy between your passbook and our records."

"I presume there will have been interest added." I suggested.

"I'm afraid Mr. Branson the discrepancy is the other way, the monthly administration fees have whittled the sum down to eighty-five dollars."

"But there was five hundred and forty-five dollars in there. I was counting in that to help me get back on my feet again."

"Be that as it may Mr. Branson the account has been

dormant for eight years and bank costs are incurred."

I could feel the blood rising in my neck. It was obvious to me that the bank manager thought he was dealing with the village idiot version of Clem Branson. He had ripped me off and I knew it. He probably assumed I would not argue and just go away with eighty-five dollars. I had learned in anger management courses in the penitentiary to remain quite calm in an argument if you want to gain the upper hand, so I said quietly,

"I want the full amount in my passbook plus five percent compounded over eight years I want it today or I will go to the state banking commission and report what this bank is doing to its clients."

The bank manager just stared at me with his mouth wide open. Finally he said perhaps under the circumstances we could make a small adjustment in your favor Mr. Branson."

Again I quietly repeated my demand and stared at him. I knew that he was well aware I had murdered a man in the past. Maybe it was fear of me on his part when he told the teller.

"Give him nine hundred and fifty dollars then get him out of here." With my prison earnings I now had eleven hundred and twenty dollars in my pockets and I was bound for California and my rendezvous with Patsy.

At the railroad depot I booked a sleeper seat on the next day's train. I wanted to arrive feeling fresh and wide awake for Patsy and I had a million things to talk about. My excitement at seeing her again mounted with each passing hour. I paid for a room in the Beantown Motel not far from the station, for dinner bought a hamburger in the coffee shop across the street. Then I hired a cab to go and have a final look at what had been the Branson family farm for three generations. The house and barn were completely gone; the land where they had stood was now bean field stubble.

It pleased me. It seemed fitting that the place that had so many bad memories for me had been obliterated. From this point on I would be free of the past and I could begin a new life with Patsy on the West Coast. Back at the Beantown Motel I realized I had no proper change of clothing or spare underwear, so I went in search of a men's wear shop, I bought an off the rack suit, shirts, socks under wear and shoes. To finish off my ensemble I bought a trilby hat like Humphrey Bogart wore. I picked up a used suitcase at a second hand store and I was ready for my next day's journey.

Stepping onto the train this time was a far cry from the last when I boarded it looking like a country bumpkin as the army called me. This time I looked and felt good, there was no fear in my heart, only a yearning to be with Patsy. I ordered good meals in the dining car; ten years of prison slop was more than enough for me. Over and over in my mind I practiced my first words to Patsy when we were finally together. I mentally wandered over passionate love scenes with her and long talks in the evenings. I would show her the photographs of my carvings in the prison chapel and she would complement and hug me. We would go to bed and completely lose ourselves in mutual need. I thought too about what kind of work I might seek, I had gained an education in the penitentiary and there were plenty of possibilities. I had long ago given up the dream of being a long haul truck driver for several reasons, one of which was my injured leg; I could not sit for long periods without it hurting. When I really thought about it I guess I just wanted to have a free hand at carving. I had learned many shortcuts while working on the chapel project and the freedom to do the work my way, had made my time pass faster and without the excruciating boredom some of my fellow convicts went through.

After a steak dinner I settled down in the sleeping car. Tomorrow at this time I would be in Patsy's arms. I did not sleep well; I lay awake wishing the night away. After an agonizingly long morning the train approached Union Station. I grabbed my bag and ran to be sure to get the very first taxi. I paid the cabbie and mounted the wide steps to the old Victorian type house. With my hands trembling I rang the doorbell. I heard footsteps approaching from inside. I was ready with my practiced words of greeting. The door opened and a woman with dark skin, probably of Mexican descent of about sixty years with a wrinkled face stood and stared at me. She wore a housewives smock over her dress and with her hair tied up in one of those handkerchief things. She looked at me inquiringly with her dark eyes. Shocked that it was not Patsy, I could say nothing. The woman continued to look at me and said,

"Whatever you are selling I don't want any. I don't buy at the door. She began to close it in my face.

"I'm looking for Patsy Branson she gave me this address," I stammered. The woman opened the door again and replied,

"She lives in the basement suite, the door is down the side of the house but she won't be in. She works for

147

the phone company and doesn't get in til about five." My elevated feelings were suddenly dashed; it had not occurred to me that she might be working and not be there to welcome me. In retrospect I had become so used to a routine of everyone being present at all times at the pen, it simply had not entered my mind. Of course she would be working, this was the real world and people had to work to earn a living.

"What time is it now?" I asked.

"Almost three o-clock. Is Mrs Branson expecting you?"

"Yes. But I have just come into the city by train; she would not know exactly when I would arrive. Would you mind if I left my suitcase here and I will go and get a meal and come back at five?" The woman agreed that I could leave the case in her hallway and pick it up later. I walked down Sutter Street for about a mile before I found a small café. My leg had begun hurting after such a strenuous walk and I decided I would take a cab back to the house just after five. I found out later that Patsy had got off work early to meet me and we had just missed each other. I hailed a passing cab and returned to the house.

I went immediately to the side door and rapped sharply. Patsy opened it. My eyes feasted upon her almost unchanged face. She looked as beautiful as the morning I left her shelling peas in the Branson farmhouse. I noticed a few worry lines that had taken up residence near her eyes and my prepared speeches flew from my brain. I burst into tears upon seeing her. She stepped up to meet me and we embraced. We stood on the doorstep our tears mingling, not a word passed between us nor needed to.

The three thousand nights we had spent apart, right at this moment were forgotten. We hugged each other like circus bears until I released my embrace and kissed Patsy's face.

"Hello Patsy." The words were a far cry from what I had intended to say.

"Hello Clem," she responded. "I did not know if you would come to me and there is so much to tell you. Are you well? Did they treat you decently in the prison?"

"Yes to both questions, Patsy. Are you well?"

"Yes Clem I'm fine but I have missed you terribly." I noticed that my suitcase had been brought to the suite and sat by the door. I went to it and opened and took out the carving of Patsy and handed it to her.

"I took it from the house that awful day and I have kept it for you ever since. It hung on a nail over my bunk and whenever I thought of you I ran my hands over it and made believe you were there with me." Patsy took my hand and led me into her bedroom. No words were needed we both knew where our immediate destinies lay. I suppose some kind of madness overtook us both. Ten years of self-denial, ten years of wishing and dreaming, ten years of forced separation came to a crashing crescendo. We rested and held each other until our feelings once again reached fever pitch and we joined in a symphony of tender loving aware only of ourselves and oblivious to the world around us.

"What are you doing to my mother?" The words shouted from the foot of the bed both shocked and baffled me. I looked down. A boy with a look of horror on his face who appeared to be about eight or nine years of age stood at the foot of the bed with a wild eyed expression.

He looked like most other boys of his age hair disheveled and wrinkled clothing with a school satchel on his back.

"Who are you? What are you doing to my mother?" He screamed again. Pasty and I separated and grabbed for the bed sheet to cover us.

"Oh my God I forgot all about the time," Patsy said. Then to the boy she said, "it's all right John he's not hurting mummy, go into the living room while I get dressed. I will explain later."

"What the Hell is going on Patsy? Who is he and why did he call you mummy?"

"Get dressed Clem we will talk about this later. Remember in the letter I wrote, I said there were issues we had to deal with?" We slipped on our clothes without another word and I followed Patsy into the living room. The boy stood by the sofa looking very confused and angry,

"Who is he Mummy? What is he doing here and why did you not have any clothes on?"

"He is my husband, John. We were married ten years ago and he has been away until today. I know this must be a big surprise to you for I have never told you about him. As for what we were doing, we were making love. This is what husbands and wives do when they love each other and we do. I should have told you a lot of things John but I didn't, and that's that."

Listening to Patsy's explanations I noticed that she had not referred to me as the boy's father. My immediate thought, so there is another man involved here. A sickening feeling lurched into my stomach; the marvelous homecoming had been stained by a shadow I knew nothing about. I looked at Patsy. Her eyes told me in no uncertain terms not to say anything right now. I gained from the look that a dark secret would be revealed to me in due course.

Did you have a good day at school John?" Patsy said in an attempt to defuse the tension between the three of us.

"Yes Mum."

"Did Mrs. Wilson make dinner for you before you left to come home?"

"Yes Mum, she made potato pancakes."

"I want you to shake hands and meet my husband, Clem. Clem was a soldier, John and he has been away since before you were born." Shyly, the boy, John approached me and we shook hands.

"How are you young man?' I said trying to be polite, but I remained as confused as Hell. Why had Patsy kept him in the dark about me? Whose child was this? I could understand the boy not knowing about love, for I too had been clueless about such matters until I went into the military. It occurred to me that it might have been better had Patsy and I corresponded more before we actually got back together. There was so much she didn't know about my life during the last ten years and apparently even more I didn't know about hers.

"Very well sir. Are you my father? All the kids at school except me have fathers," the child responded. I had not a clue how to answer the boy so I said,

"All the kids?"

"Well except Janice Morton, her daddy got dead in the war. That was her real daddy, she has another one now." I knew I had to steer the conversation away from our relationship, or lack of it so I said.

"Many children lost their father's in the war John. I was there and saw many young fathers die. I got shot in the legs and came home to America." I realized I came close to saying too much so I left it there.

"Did it hurt a lot, being shot?"

"Yes John, it hurt an awful lot, but I was lucky, I am still alive."

Patsy came to my rescue,

"Get ready for bed now John. Clem and I have a lot of things to talk about."

Patsy helped him get ready for bed, while I sat on the sofa dreading what I would learn and how it might affect my life. The initial dream of my homecoming had already been shattered despite the magnificent first couple of hours. I could not help but wonder if it would be possible to get back to the idyllic love we had shared ten years earlier. I hoped it would, but the knotted feeling in my gut told a different story.

"I'm going to make a pot of coffee Clem. Do you still drink it black with no sugar?" Patsy offered, when the boy had been put to bed.

"Yes please Patsy." I wondered how the projected conversation would begin. Would I ask, or would she tell. In a few minutes, Patsy brought two cups of steaming coffee and sat down across from me. There was an awkward silence, then after taking a sip from her cup, Patsy began to speak.

"There is so much that you do not know Clem Branson." Patsy's eyes began to tear up as she forced the words out. I knew when she used my surname I should listen without interrupting.

"On that awful day ten years ago I ran past you on

the road because I believe I went temporarily insane after your father so violently raped me. The only thing I could think to do was run and I kept on running then I left the road and hid among some trees. I spent the night there and crept back to the farm in the morning hoping to find you. But you were not there and when I found all the blood in the house I thought your father must have killed you and taken your body away.

I was terrified that he may still be around waiting to kill me next, so I put on some clothes and walked all the way into town. It was there that I discovered that it was you who had killed him and then turned yourself into the Sheriff. They would not let me see you, so I could not tell you what exactly had occurred nor hear your story. I assume you killed him in revenge for raping me Clem. I know you did it because you loved me and could not bear to see me hurt." Patsy began to sob as she continued to tell me her story.

I went to the pastor of your old church and asked him for help since I had no money and I did not want to return to the farm. He allowed me to stay for one night, but I could tell he thought I was an unsavory person I'm sure he thought I was lying when I told him your father had raped me. He told me to go back to the farm; he said it was what you would have wanted. I hitched a ride with a neighboring farmer and he made moves on me." Patsy began to sob again. I reached out and took her hand but kept silent waiting for her to begin again.

"I knew I could not leave Gage County until after your trial. When I began to run out of groceries I managed to drive the truck into the bean co-op. They refused to allow me to charge anything since the account was in your father's name and he had been murdered. On the way home a deputy stopped me and impounded the truck and gave me a ticket, which I could not pay. I had to walk back, it was too far to walk to town each day to get work so I managed by eating the loose beans left in the silos after the co-op emptied them.

I did see you in the court, but I could not speak to you privately to tell you how I felt or what was happening in my life. The authorities said I could visit you in the penitentiary after you had been in for thirty days. I do not know how I survived those thirty days Clem, then I had to hitch hike to Watson County to see you." Patsy let out a huge sob and I went to my knees to hold her as she wept. When the shaking of her body slowed she continued,

"It was there that you broke my heart Clem Branson. I bore a terrible secret and I needed to confide in you, but you told me to go and make a new life for myself. You were thinking about your feelings, Clem not mine. For me it was the last straw, two months of utter Hell and you dismissed me like a schoolgirl. I left the prison and immediately began hitch hiking to San Francisco without a penny in my purse I looked up my old friend Margery and she took me in and assisted me in getting on my feet again. I moved into here, when she married and went to live in San Diego."

I held Patsy close and stroked her soft hair.

"My darling Patsy, I had no idea that you suffered so. Yes you are right, I was thinking of my own feelings. But I thought that I might spare yours by freeing you to go your own way. If only you had written to me?"

"Clem! If I had written you telling you of my troubles

you could not have helped me in any way, it would have served only to make you suffer too. It may sound trite and even stupid but I did not contact you because I loved you. I am also aware that you would have had no idea where I was and until I read about your pardon in the paper, it would have stayed that way for both our sakes."

Patsy ceased talking and sat looking downcast. Her words had indicated that she had loved me all along just as I had loved her, but it did not explain the boy sleeping in the next room who called her mother. I wondered if in her loneliness she had adopted him and I was loath to ask, I felt she would soon tell me when the right moment presented itself.

"What about you Clem? How did you survive incarceration?"

"Apart from missing you terribly Patsy, it was quite tolerable. They said I was a model prisoner and asked me how they could make things easier for me. I told them I would like to get back to carving and to make a long story short I carved just about every piece of wood in the prison chapel. When the State Governor saw my work and prison records, he recommended a pardon and here I am a free man sitting with the woman I love more than life itself. Before I caught the train I made a visit out to the Branson farmstead it had been bulldozed down and the place is now a bean field. I felt happy to see it gone, for now I can put aside all the bad memories of it and my father. You know Patsy, in all the years I knew my father, I never once saw him smile.

"I saw your father smile once Clem. It was an evil smile. Kind of like a cat having finished off a rat. Through the smile he drooled tobacco juice down my neck and chest as he raped me. His foul breath haunts me still. I'm glad you killed him Clem, but you didn't deserve the sentence you got for it. At this point you have no inkling of the punishment I also received for his actions; in some ways mine was worse than yours. In your case it was all over when your knife ended his life. My punishment was just beginning from beyond the grave."

"What do you mean Patsy? I don't understand." The tears began again as Patsy sat up straight and looked me in the eye, and began by asking me a question.

"Do you remember Clem how we were always so careful that I didn't become pregnant when we were first married?"

"Yes Patsy I remember." I waited for her to continue, wondering where she was taking the conversation.

"Your father took no such precautions when he raped me Clem. He was foul, brutal and he left his seed in me." Patsy paused waiting for my reaction. I must still have had some of the country bumpkin in me for I didn't comprehend what Patsy was telling me. She stared at me and I stared back confused. After a few moments silence, Patsy blurted out.

"Jesus Christ Clem! Your father made me pregnant. The boy in the other room is your father's son! He is your half brother, Clem. Don't you understand? That is what I meant in my letter that we have issues to deal with!"

I felt my blood rising up in my neck just the way I remember it had the day I killed my father. My throat seized up. I could not speak and the same kind of madness that had come over me on that day ten years ago came over me again. I felt that even the killing of my father had not stopped his evil influence over me. Was the boy the reincarnation of my father? Was I destined to kill him too? I felt the best thing I could do at the moment would be to get out of the suite as soon as possible for I could not face life in prison or the electric chair if I killed the boy in the state I was in at the moment. I leapt to my feet, grabbed my jacket off the chair back and ran out to the street. I felt no pain in my leg as I ran. My limbs were deadened by the thoughts surging through my brain. I remember running down Sutter Street then all the way down to the harbor front. I must have had suicide on my mind for I found myself on the Golden Gate Bridge looking down into the swiftly running tide. It would be so easy to be rid of the memory of my father and his evilness, two seconds to climb the rail and ten more to hit the concrete like surface of the water. It would all be over.

An outward-bound freighter passed directly below me. I could not jump now. Looking back on that moment, I know the freighter saved my life, for it gave me a few seconds to reconsider what I had been about to do. I thought about Patsy and how just hours before we had shared the ecstasy of our renewed lovemaking. Would I allow my father, reincarnated or not take that from me again? Calmer now I realized I had run from Patsy in a state of mild madness, just as she had run from me that fatal day ten years ago. I owed it to her to allow her to fully explain the circumstances surrounding the child, my half brother, and my father's son. I had no idea if I could accept the boy as part of our renewed family. Perhaps I would hate him for what and whom he represented.

I began walking back in the direction of San Francisco. Now that a semblance of sanity had returned,

I realized how much I had damaged my war wound with the running. The pain was excruciating and I limped exceedingly slowly to the end of the bridge. I managed to hail a cab and returned to the suite. Patsy answered my knock on her door with a look of utter dejection on her tear stained face.

"I'm sorry I ran out Patsy, the shock was too great for me to handle. Now I understand why you ran so hard and long after my father attacked you. I had the feeling that my father had reached out from the grave to continue his malevolence against me. Obviously I had no idea of the trauma you must have felt knowing you were to have his child and with me locked away unable to offer any emotional support. Yes Patsy, you are right there are issues we have to deal with."

I felt for her hand and together we walked into the living room and sat down.

"Talk to me Patsy, spill it all out and then we can deal with the issues facing us." Hesitantly, Patsy began to speak.

"As I told you Clem, I knew I was pregnant when I came to visit you in the penitentiary. You gave me no opportunity to tell you and I knew I had to bear the pregnancy and the shame of motherhood alone without a husband. I knew that in the religious community of Gage County I could never get the pregnancy terminated, even if it were possible I had no money and no opportunity to earn any. I was forced by the actions of your father to carry to term the child growing within me. A child I grew to hate even though it was unborn. Every single day my own body reminded me of Jed Branson his meanness, his vile attitude, his disgusting habit of spitting after chewing tobacco and most of all his brutal attack, holding me down while he performed his immoral act upon me. I planned to give the child up for adoption at the moment of birth, for I didn't believe I could offer any kind of love to your father's spawn. When he actually came into the world I couldn't bear to look at the child's face in case it was a replica of your father's.

The delivery nurse coaxed me into looking at him after she had placed him in my arms; through one eye I saw not your father's face Clem, but yours. Suddenly my whole world changed, this child had grown and developed within my body, the child was a part of my body until the moment he arrived. I knew instantly I could not give him away, even though he was indeed, Jed Branson's son. I have learned to look past that awful fact Clem. John is my son and I love him as my son. I will raise him as my son. So you see my dear husband, John and I are a package deal. If you want me in your life you must accept John as part of it. That, Clem, is the issue we have to deal with.

We love each other Clem. I have never doubted my love for you even for a moment and apart from the day I visited you in prison, I have never doubted your love for me. But a third and then a fourth party came between our love, namely your father first and then my son. Do I want you in my life Clem? Yes I do. I know you want me in yours, but do you want John?"

Patsy fell silent. I knew she awaited my response, but right then and there I could not answer her truthfully.

"Yes Patsy, I do want you in my life. I will try my best to make John a part of our lives, but you must realize that it will take some time for me to get completely used

159

to the idea. It has been an awful shock to me tonight, so unexpected and the news so distressing."

"I have to work in the morning Clem. I have to get some rest or I shall be useless tomorrow, come to bed." We did go to bed and it was wonderful to have Patsy lying beside me. We were both too exhausted to become physical and my leg hurt quite badly, but despite the nagging pain I slept and I had the dream for the first time. It was to be the first episode of a recurring dream one that came to me quite regularly, one that I could not tell Patsy about even though we had no other secrets between us.

The alarm clock shattered the quiet of the morning with a raucous ringing.

"You stay here while I make breakfast Clem. I'll call you when it is on the table." It was a simple meal of cold cereal and sourdough bread toasted with strawberry jam and coffee. John sat across the table from me and I silently watched him eating, to see if I could recognize any of my father's traits in his facial expressions.

"What will you do today while I am at work Clem?"

"I think I should stay here. My leg still hurts from over exerting it yesterday, and then tomorrow I should think about getting some kind of work."

"If you are going to be here in the suite Clem, then John can come straight home from school instead of going to the child-minders until I get off work. That way you can get to know each other. I'm sure you can find something in the fridge for your lunch and I will make dinner for us when I get home." She and the boy left and I had an entire day to think about the last twenty-four hours. Used to the dull never changing routine of prison life, the revelations of yesterday had left me drained and confused. There had been way too much information to absorb so quickly.

I lay back on the sofa with my bad leg hanging over the edge with my right foot resting on the floor. Feeling relatively comfortable I allowed my mind to wander at will. It took me back to the Branson bean farm to my mother and my father's ill treatment of her. I tried to make sense of it but I couldn't. They were man and wife as Patsy and I were; yet I never saw even the most remote act of love or tenderness from my father. There had to be something wrong there, but what? Surely there had to have been love of some sort at one time in their married life or they would have never married in the first place? The wondering led to my grandparents, were they too not totally lacking in love for each other? I of course had no knowledge of my great grandparents, but the little I did know suggested that they too had little respect or love for each other. Why were the Branson men like this? Like the religious gobbledygook my father used to prate about, I didn't believe in curses. I mean the kind of curse that is carried on between generations. So far as I knew I had not inherited the traits of my ancestors via the Branson curse.

Such an idea was ridiculous but my mind had taken me there. By getting away from the Branson farm influence and joining the military had I broken the supposed curse? As my mind toyed with the idea I realized that by murdering my father maybe I had. But I acted out the curse in a different more violent way.

I remembered that in anger management classes at the penitentiary the instructor had spoken about violent events repeating themselves, just as history often repeated itself and I could not help but wonder if in the grand scheme of things that I too was part of such a circle of cruelty? Again had my leaving the farm behind broken the circle? Had the generational penchant for cruelty been split asunder?

I had no answers for my own questions and so my mind took off on a different tack. Though it pained me, I began to think of Patsy's rape. My eyes moistened at the thought of my father forcing himself upon her, for I too had suffered under his hand when too weak and small to defend myself against his cruelty. My suffering had been confined to beatings and verbal abuse but Patsy's went far beyond what I had known. My father had forced his way into the temple of her body inflicting not only physical pain but also deep psychological distress. He had also impregnated her causing excruciating emotional pain and forcing her to have an unwanted child. I have never regretted killing him; as far as I was concerned he more than deserved it.

This thought led me back to my previous one. Was it father's intent to continue the circle of violence by raping Patsy, with the circle to be continued by the child she would bear? It occurred to me that if this indeed was the case, Patsy had been brought within the circle while I had been ejected from it by my leaving the farm environment and learning a new way of life in the military. This would have been obvious to father on the very day I arrived back with my bride when we fought outside the house porch. But how about Patsy, she too had changed her life since leaving the farm? I could make no sense of the thoughts invading my head; possibly it was an odd reaction to yesterday's news.

I changed my thinking to the boy, John. I wondered why Patsy had named him John. I reasoned she had because she certainly couldn't have called him, Clement and definitely not Jeddadiah. Possibly it had been one of her relative's names. I could not help wondering if the circle of violence had been bred into the child and it might develop in later life like some macabre disease. I had learned while in prison that human genetics while still a fairly new science in the early fifties, showed positive results that certain traits could be passed from generation to generation with no way to prevent it from happening. Could this be the case with the boy? But then I reasoned if it were, then the same traits would still be within me too.

I quickly dispelled my own argument, for I knew that violence did not lurk within me. With my mind somewhat calmed and my leg comfortable, I fell asleep. I slept until about noon then I made a sandwich and a cup of tea from things I found in the small kitchen. I figured I would get some exercise by going to buy a newspaper to look for work in the want ads. I went back to the suite with a copy of the San Francisco Chronicle and looked through the help wanted ads. I found an ad for a stone carver for a monument company. I had never worked with stone before, but apart from different tools and working material it might be something I could do. After all carving was an art form I was familiar with and I could but ask. I pulled my portfolio of photographs of the prison chapel carvings from my suitcase; I would show them to Patsy and John later. I went back out again to find a pay phone and made an appointment with the

163

monument company for tomorrow morning.

John came home just after three-thirty. I felt very uncomfortable with him. Never having had a brother I had no idea how to be brotherly with him nor could I be fatherly, I had neither the right nor the inclination. The boy was under the impression I had just come from duty in the military, Patsy had not told him yet that I had spent the last ten years in prison so it was with some relief when he asked about my life in the army. Telling the boy the truth about me, our relationship and the circumstances of his birth was another issue that Patsy and I had to face together. I answered all his questions about the military and he seemed bright and well able to understand what I had been telling him. I watched him carefully as we talked looking for any sign that he might resemble my father. Also I could not help but wonder about the things that had passed through my mind this morning.

Patsy arrived home about five pm.

"How did you and John get along this afternoon Clem?"

"Just fine Patsy, he wanted to know about life in the army and my war experiences. Guess what? I have a job interview tomorrow for a stone carver for a monument company. I dug out my pictorial carving reference. Come and take a look."

"You did all this Clem." Patsy exclaimed after viewing the pictures of the chapel carvings. "Will you tell them that you are newly released from the uh uh, Clem?" She said nodding in John's direction.

"Not unless they insist. Then I will tell them I was commissioned by the state to carve the chapel."

"Have you started your homework John?" Patsy

asked him. The boy screwed up his face in annoyance and then I saw it. The narrow rat like eyes glared at his mother and his lips tightly pursed uttered the words,

"No I haven't. Not yet. I was talking with Clem." There was no mistaking it. It was a miniature of my father's face complete with a hint of the cruelty he had possessed. My heart missed a beat; perhaps the boy was a reincarnation of my father, just as I had thought earlier. I wondered if in later years the boy would wreak misery on another generation of Branson's. He may even cause great distress to his own mother Patsy, or even become a reason to come between her and I.

"Go and do your homework John, I will call you when supper is ready," Patsy chided. When he had left the room I said to Patsy,

"How are we going to explain to him where I have been and who he really is Patsy? At this point he probably thinks I am his father returned from military duty. If he wishes to think it and call me father, it will be O.K. with me, but sooner or later he has to know the truth."

"I have kept the truth from him for obvious reasons Clem. No child would want to admit to his classmates that his father is a jailbird. Even though technically you are not his father, surely you are not suggesting that I tell him he arrived in the world basically unwanted because a degenerate raped his mother? Had you been here all along Clem, we would not have this dilemma." She said sharply.

"There is no need to get annoyed Patsy. You know damn well I would have been here for the both of you, unfortunately the State saw things differently."

"How can you ask me not to get angry Clem? You

show up here after ten damn years and start by telling me what to do. Had you been in my position would you have done things differently? I have sweat blood and tears to raise the child alone and raise him well. I won't go into the unholy conception we both know what happened. So don't come the Jed Branson with me, telling me what I should do or not do!" Patsy stormed off into the kitchen.

She had never spoken to me in such a tone before. I could not help but think of the things that had run through my mind this morning. Had my father's actions brought Patsy within the circle? Had he by planting his evil seed in her somehow infected her with the morose and violent attitude of himself? Was this attitude manifesting its scorpion sting towards me, now that I was on the scene again? On the other hand I thought perhaps she felt tired after a stressful night and a day at work with little sleep. Maybe I had just rubbed her the wrong way and spoke without thinking. I went to the kitchen and said,

"I'm sorry Patsy. I didn't mean to hurt or upset you I have been away from you so long I have forgotten how to be sweet and kind. Please forgive me?" Patsy came to me and we hugged.

"I brought us pork chops would you like one or two?"

"Two" I replied. The little tiff was over.

CHAPTER EIGHT.

"Come into the office," he said when I introduced myself to the owner of the monument company. He was not the suit and tie kind of owner, he was a hands on kind of fellow who worked in dust covered clothing alongside his employees. He had the rugged appearance of a man who had seen a lot of life. He wore a baseball cap badly worn and coated with years of granite and marble dust cemented onto the fabric with rainwater. His face weathered and tanned from working out in the California sun, sported bushy eyebrows having a fine coating of fresh marble dust that flew off the air-powered chisel he had held in his knarled hands when I first approached him. The office was just as dust covered as his clothing, unclaimed grave markers leaned against the walls and a host of nails held papers in profusion around the walls. His desk looked like it could use a hosepipe on it as opposed to tidying it up.

"I'm George Nelson. I own this place, took over from my father when I got back from Europe after the war.

You said on the phone that you had carving experience; let me have a look at your work." I showed him my portfolio of carvings. "That's pretty damn good. What's your name again?"

"Clem Sir. Clem Branson."

"Don't call me Sir. The Goddamn war is over and I'm done with the Sir crap. Every body calls me George and it suits me fine. It's plain to see you have good skills working with wood. Stone and marble are a different kettle of fish. I can start you off working at simple lettering on headstones, that way you will know if the job will suit you and if you will suit me. Come in at eight in the morning and I will start you off at two bucks per hour. Once in a while we are asked about wood carving by church ministers, if I am asked again I can let you see the plans and quote the time needed on the job. It could be done under my company name. See you in the morning Clem."

I left the premises and figured I should buy some sturdy work clothes. I took a bus down to Market Street and picked up some tough denim pants and shirt, a shower-proof jacket and some high work boots. In Woolworth's I bought a tin lunch bucket complete with a thermos bottle. On a whim I entered a knife and cutlery shop and bought young John a whittling knife. At a corner grocery near the suite I picked a bunch of flowers out of a bucket for Patsy.

"Thank you Clem they are lovely. I can't remember the last time I had any flowers," she said when she came home from work.

"I have a gift for you too John. My mother bought me one of these many years ago. I will bring some scraps of wood home tomorrow and show you how to use it." John didn't thank me verbally for the knife, he just grunted. I had expected him to be excited just as I had been, the thoughts I had about him yesterday flew back into my mind. His attitude was the same as my father's had been when I presented him with one of my little gifts. I asked myself again could the boy be a reincarnation of my father? Was such a thing possible? I kept my thoughts to myself knowing I had to learn to accept John, if Patsy and I were to have a life together.

"I start work tomorrow." I announced during dinner. "At the monument company. The boss, George is going to start me off carving names on headstones. I will be using an air powered chisel instead of my old hand tools. With us both working, after a while we can afford a few luxuries."

"Such as?" Patsy asked.

"Better clothes, a used car, maybe in the future we can buy our own house with a garden."

"A garden! If you think for one minute Clem Branson, that you are going to have me slaving in the hot sun hoeing vegetables like on that Goddamn farm, You had best think again!"

I could not for the life of me think why Patsy would suddenly take such offense; I was expounding an idea, not laying down the law. Her behaviour was so unlike the Patsy of ten years ago. My thoughts returned to the circle I had thought about earlier, had she been drawn in? Was her sharpness the start of a life like my father's had been? A life where nothing seemed to please and acidic responses were the norm?

"Of course not Patsy. I was thinking of you having

your very own house and a yard for John to play ball. Not to turn you into a farmhand."

"Oh," she replied. Once again I had defused the situation, but I could not help but wonder how often her attitude would suddenly change. Conversation during the meal became somewhat subdued. I had felt great excitement at finding work so quickly and had wished to share my enthusiasm with Patsy, but as a result of her questioning attitude, I said no more about it.

I had the dream again during the night and I woke up sweating and with my heart racing. I sat up in bed and in the light from the street lamp filtering through the drapes, I saw Patsy, sleeping soundly beside me. The dream was so disturbing I failed to go back to sleep and lay waiting for the alarm to go off at seven. After a quick breakfast we all went our separate ways John to the child minders until it was time for school, Patsy to her job and I to mine carrying my new lunch pail.

George Nelson handed me a cup of coffee in a badly stained mug.

"I'll get you started after coffee," he said. He took me to a rough workbench outside under a rudimentary roof. "Let's see how you do with this Clem." A slab of granite lay on the bench with the words IN LOVING MEMORY penciled neatly across the top. "This is your air chisel Clem. Steady your arm and work slowly letting the chisel do the cutting for you." George demonstrated how the job was done then handed me the tool. I found it rather odd at first the chisel seemed to want to wander, but I held it between the pencil lines and soon I had a quarter inch deep vee shaped letter I. George came to inspect it and gave me the go ahead to continue.

Despite the noise of the chisel and the dust it created I soon found that I could guide the chisel and allow my mind to wander at will. I thought about the words I was in the process of carving. The only loving memory I could think of was of my mother. I remembered how there was no such headstone for her. My father would never have spent the money for such a frivolity as he called almost everything that had no direct bearing on the farm. My thoughts returned to the idea of a circle and I wondered if my grandparents were the beginning of the circle, or did it go back much further than them. Was it genetic or a learned trait?

The more I thought about the idea of the circle the more convinced I became that it did in fact exist. I wondered if my grandfather had committed the same act upon my mother as my father had perpetrated on Patsy. Perhaps this was the reason my father had hated me for as long as I can remember. If the hypothesis was true then it was no wonder he held me at arms length. I supposed it was possible the trait went far back into the family history. I began to consider that perhaps my kin was cursed or inhabited by demons having the ability to transfer from father to grandson. Could it be the religious fervor displayed by family members was a desperate but failed attempt to hold the demons at bay? Could the act of rape perpetrated upon a young female be the vehicle of transfer for the evil beings? If any of this was true where did it leave me? Did the demons live quietly within me waiting for the moment to drive me over the edge? But had I not already committed murder and felt no regrets for the crime? I thought I had broken out of the circle but now I really wasn't sure, perhaps I was still very much a part of it.

"Coffee break Clem!" the words jolted me back from my thoughts. "You are doing a fine job Clem, its time to take a breather." I looked at my block of granite, now that my mind was cleared of family matters; I saw I had almost finished. The letters were a deep vee and straight as a die. After the break I went back and finished the lettering, George was pleased with the results.

"Now we will put you to the real test Clem." He brought out a metal template of an angel with wings. "Put this on your slab Clem and draw your pencil lines around it then carve me an angel, then we will know if you really are a carver."

I placed the template and drew around it and began to carve the basic shape into the granite. Since George had not been specific I began to create my own version within the confines of the drawing. By the end of the day George was highly pleased with the results. As for myself the concentration on the job at hand had given me relief from the thoughts that had invaded my mind earlier.

"How did your day go Clem?" Patsy asked when I walked in.

"Fine. The boss seemed pleased with me. Working with an air chisel takes a bit of getting used to, but once I got the hang of it, it proved to be a versatile tool.

"Do you think you will like working there Clem?"

"Yes I think I will. George seems to leave me room to use my own imagination within the framework of a headstone." Patsy served dinner and John joined us at the table. Taking care not to stare I watched him as he ate; many of his mannerisms reminded me of my father and the way he had behaved at the table. My thoughts of earlier in the day returned. I wondered if my father's spirit lived within the boy, perhaps when he was old enough the boy might exact my father's revenge upon me by killing me just as I had killed my father. Could it be a circle within a circle? I resolved that I would have to become wary of the boy as time went by.

"You are very quiet Clem, are you tired after the first day on the job?" Not wishing to voice my thoughts to Patsy I replied,

"Yes. I think I am," I said looking up at her. Maybe it was just the glance, but I saw a different Patsy. Just for an instant I thought I saw my father's eyes in hers. Maybe he had infected her as I had wondered earlier. In an odd sort of way my world had begun to unravel. The steady unchanging life in the Penitentiary had been replaced by daily challenges I was unused to. The exquisite anticipation of re-uniting with Patsy had been tempered by the revelations of recent days. Knowing the boy was my father's offspring weighed heavily upon me. Strange thoughts were invading my mind and I could discuss them with no one. The magic, Patsy and I had shared ten years ago no longer existed. I still loved her, but now I felt that something sinister had come between us. Then there was that awful recurring dream, it troubled me greatly and I wondered if the dream was a warning of things to come.

Deep in thought I had not noticed that John had left the table.

"Is it the boy that is troubling you so Clem?" Patsy's inquiring voice grabbed my attention and brought me back to the here and now. "Is knowing John is not your son, causing your melancholy Clem? Are you not ready to accept him as I have accepted him? This is an issue we have to deal with if we are to remain living together as man and wife. You have to remember Clem the boy is blameless, he is an innocent victim of the violence of another person surely you can see that?" Patsy had forced me into responding when I really didn't feel like it.

"Yes. I have to admit Patsy, the boy disturbs me. It could be that is because I don't know him like you do. He is a whole new figure in my life and I have not adjusted to him yet. Yes I realize he is innocent in the circumstances of his birth but I have to be honest with you Patsy, at certain times I see my father's face in his. It seems to be mocking me as though my father had the last word through him." I watched Patsy's face twist into anger. I knew it would happen if I told her the truth.

"Being in prison has bent your mind Clem Branson. You must have been sitting in there day after day thinking about your rotten childhood and the death of your miserable father. It's time to get over it and get on with building a new life, if not with my son and I, then on your own." Patsy's voice raised a few decibels. "Do not even think about asking me to choose between you or he, Clem Branson for it will never happen. John is part of me and I am part of him. In reality you are not part of the picture. Do not think that after ten years of struggling on my own that you can come here and expect me to change everything just to please you. The circumstances being what they are, it is you who has to change. If you are not willing to do that I suggest you find a place to live alone until you are ready to accept John as your son or make a new life for yourself."

Now my temper began to rise.

"Are you telling me to leave Patsy? Yes I've had ten years to ruminate on things past how could it have been otherwise? But I never stopped loving you as you seem to have stopped feeling the same way about me." I considered telling her about the thoughts I had been having but thought better of it for the moment. "You must admit it was a Hell of a shock to find out about John, how did you expect me to react? Did you think I would be overjoyed? Had it been anyone other than my father who had raped you it would have been better than this."

"Now you are saying my being raped would have been O.K. with you if it had been a total stranger. That is a strange statement from one who claims to love me. You know what Clem; I think you had better leave. I got along before you showed up again and I will get along after you have gone." By now our voices were raised to the point where we were shouting at each other and all reason had been cast aside.

"Then I'll go Patsy. It is obvious you no longer have feelings for me." I stomped around the suite gathering my things and slammed the door on the way out. I found a crummy room in a seedy downtown hotel and lay on the bed thinking about my day and how it had ended with us being apart. Melancholy descended upon me and my thoughts of earlier in the day returned. I became increasingly convinced that Patsy had indeed become infected by the Branson curse. Why else would she have defended the boy so strongly and why had she suggested that I leave so soon after we had been reunited? I was sure now that my father's evil ways had been transferred to both Patsy and her child. Now he could reach out and torture me from beyond the grave.

I had been safe from his influence while in the penitentiary, but now things had changed. The vivid dream I had been having of killing both Patsy, and the boy, suddenly made sense. It would be the only way to break the circle if both of them were dead; the Branson curse would die with them. Not only that, but I would be freeing them both of a life of dispensing misery to others and myself. I would in effect be doing both of them a favor.

Of course I knew that if I did kill them both I would be the immediate suspect and face even more time in the penitentiary. But I felt that even if it did happen, my time would not be quite so bad, because I would not miss Patsy this time knowing I had done the loving thing for her and the boy. I would have broken the circle and I too would now be free of it.

I got up from the bed and decided I would go for a drink. I hadn't had a beer since I left the army. In a tavern down the block I ordered my first beer then my second and third. I had thought that having a few beers would take away the macabre thoughts crossing my mind much like traffic through an intersection. The fact is it intensified them. After my sixth beer my mind became numb and I staggered back to my hotel room and went to sleep fully dressed. The noise of city traffic woke me and daylight streamed through the dirty glass panes of the window overlooking a squalid back alley.

I went down to the lobby to ask the time and I deduced that by the time I got to my job I would be almost an hour late.

"Late on your second day on the job Clem! This better be the last time. I can't do with tardy employees. Next time you figure you are going to be late, don't bother coming back. You didn't tell me you were a drinker. But I'll tell you this, I won't put up with it, whether you are a good carver or not."

"I'm sorry George." I said I am not a drinker as you put it; last night was the first time in over ten years. My wife and I had a quarrel and I sipped a few beers. It won't happen again."

"See that it doesn't Clem. What you do on your own time is your affair, but when it encroaches on mine it's my business, now go and finish the work you began yesterday."

I began working on the granite angel; the flying dust dried my already dry mouth even more. I was dying for a mug of coffee, I had not had any breakfast nor had I brought a lunch. I told myself I would not do any more drinking during the week. Despite my pounding head I produced a carving that pleased George and I felt I had redeemed myself. We took the slab of carved granite and leaned it against a wall. It needed only a date and name adding when a customer ordered a headstone.

"Clem! I would like you to work on a special order. It's a big job but I have confidence you can handle it. I have only a rough drawing of what the customer wants so you will be working freehand. It is a three dimensional monument it has to look good from every angle take your time and get it right."

The overhead crane delivered a huge block of granite to my workstation and I began to draw the first rough outlines of what materiel had to be chiseled away. George was as good as his word and left me alone to do the job my way. Thinking about the project kept me from dwelling .

on my family problems and by Friday night I had calmed down to a large degree. I stopped in at a used car lot on the way home from work and purchased a 1938 dodge four door car. One hundred and fifty dollars bought me a solid car with a few bumps and scrapes on the fenders. It felt so good to be behind the wheel again.

I though I would stop by Patsy's place and offer to take her and the boy for a ride around the Bay area. Patsy too had got over her anger and readily agreed to accompany me.

"Don't bother cooking a dinner Patsy; we will buy something while we are out."

We drove out to the Pacific shore and bought hamburgers and a coke each at a drive in. We sat in the car eating, when I glanced in the mirror and saw John staring out of the window as he ate his burger, the likeness to my father was startling. I almost choked on my food so I took a gulp of my coke to stop my coughing.

"Is something the matter Clem?" Patsy inquired. I lied and said,

"No. I just took too big of a bite." I knew now for sure that I had to somehow deal with the boy it was the only way to break the circle and free him from the evil lurking inside. But I would have to plan things very carefully. I said nothing of my thoughts to Patsy and we continued on our tour of the San Francisco area.

"Do you want to continue living in that hotel Clem? Or do you want to live with me and John."

"I hate the hotel Patsy; I would rather live with you. I realize that things are different for us now but I will try to adjust if you will try to be understanding of me and my ways. I thought it would be easy to adjust from the dull routine of prison life but it isn't."

"I will try Clem, if you will. Drop by your hotel and pick up your things and come back home." Patsy stroked her hand on my knee and I knew she wanted me. Memories of that day in the bean field in the warm sun where we loved each other with wild abandon surged into my mind pushing out the earlier macabre thoughts. For a couple of hours after John had gone to sleep it was as if nothing had ever gone wrong between us. The passion of our newlywed bliss returned and we became lost in each other's arms. Just before I succumbed to sleep I remember thinking how great it would be if this feeling of utter contentment were to last.

A new day dawned. We went to our respective jobs, John to school. I had begun to enjoy the artistic freedom I had at the monument company. George Nelson left me alone to create whatever I wanted within the parameters of the blocks of granite. Having the freedom to a large degree kept my mind clear of the thoughts I had been having. Both Patsy and I tried our best to accommodate our small differences. I kept my mouth shut regarding the boy, but the occasional glimpse of my father in his facial expressions slowly but surely created and built a simmering volcano of ill feelings in my breast toward him. There were times when I felt I should like to strike him, but I held the feelings in check, for not to do so would place me at the same level as my father had been with me.

"You are not warming up to John, very well Clem." Patsy admonished after a few weeks of relative calm.

"I'm doing my best." I snapped back.

"Your best isn't very good Clem. I am not blind. I see

how you look at him sometimes. There is almost hatred in your eyes. The circumstances of his conception were not of his doing. He is blameless Clem can't you get it through your thick country bumpkin head?"

I had not been called a country bumpkin since my induction into the army a dozen or so years earlier. The anger that I had successfully held back then, now broke loose.

"Who do you think you are Patsy? You didn't mind me being a country bumpkin when we married and went to live in Gage County. I admit I may have been one once, but that was long before we met. Where do you think insults are going to get you Patsy? It seems I was right in my thinking that you have become infected with my father's evilness, just as you in turn have infected the boy. It's plain to see in his face when he looks a certain way, at others when he is eating. The boy is the reincarnation of my father can you not see that Patsy?"

"You are crazy Clem Branson! Your time behind bars has warped your thinking. If anyone is the reincarnation of Jed Branson It is you Clem! Your old man spent years indoctrinating you with his disgusting and twisted mind. It is you who has been infected, as you call it with his evilness, not my son who incidentally happens to be your Goddamn brother." Our voices had now reached the screaming point. Of course I knew I was right. Patsy was attempting to shield both her and the boy from the truth.

"Face the facts Patsy! The moment my father thrust his evil seed into you, you became a different person. Didn't you run past me on the road and hide from me? Didn't you stay hidden until I had murdered him? It was because he had taken over your body with the power of his evil Patsy. I remember the pastor saying that the devil works in mysterious ways. I believe my family has been infected with the devils evil going back several generations. I have given this a lot of thought Patsy; I believe it has been transferred to both you and the boy."

"You really are crazy Clem! I have never heard such garbage in my entire life and believe me I've heard a lot. Frankly I think you should go and see a doctor!"

"You are being insulting again Patsy! It is you who should take the boy and go to the church for an exorcism. Only then will you be rid of the evil living within you."

"If there is evil in any of us Clem, it is in you. Can't you see how distorted your thinking has become? How can you possibly think John is evil? He is just a boy doing boy things, thinking and acting like a normal boy. A completely different childhood than your own of beatings, bible thumping, rejection and child labour on a loveless bean farm in God forsaken Gage County!"

"Yes I had a hard life as a youngster, but it made me strong, able to think for myself. Somehow the Branson curse of evil by-passed both mother and I. But I have no doubt in my mind that it has been transferred to both of you!" At this point the landlady upstairs began banging on the floor in order to quiet us down.

"You moron Clem, you will get us evicted if you don't quit your yelling."

"You are yelling just as loud, you stupid bitch. I'll quiet down when you agree to go and seek an exorcism for you and the boy!" I suppose Patsy had just about enough and she began to cry. Of course being infected with the Branson evil she was unwilling to see the truth

181

in what I had told her. At that moment we both saw John standing by his bedroom door wide eyed and appearing frightened having been woken by the altercation. I stared at him and saw without a doubt in my mind the face of my father and I remembered how I never saw him smile.

Now that my feelings and convictions were out in the open between Patsy and I, our relationship began to go downhill. She refused to go with the boy to seek out having an exorcism, while I was convinced it was the only thing that could save both of them from a future of evil and the prospects of our marriage. Patsy refused to sleep in the same bed and took to sleeping on the chesterfield.

Conversation between the boy and I was minimal. It appeared to me that he considered me to be an interloper into his and his mother's lives. He would stare at me with a kind of disdain that reminded me of the way my father used to look at me. This attitude convinced me even more that he possessed the Branson curse and would wreak havoc on God only knows how many lives in the future. There was only one solution, the same one that I had in my dreams. The boy had to die. I wondered perhaps when I killed him, his mother would be released from the curse and we could rekindle the closeness we had once shared.

I had to figure out how I would relieve him of the blight. Drowning or a knife the way I had killed my father, or by bludgeoning him. The more I thought about it I realized I would have to make the death seem like an accident. I knew instinctively that Patsy would not understand what a great favor I had done her. If I were to renew our closeness it would have to appear that I had no hand in his demise.

I went daily to my job at the monument company, I had mastered the air chisel and could work without too much concentration and it allowed me to try to think of how I would dispatch John. The atmosphere at home was tense and acidic for the most part. I suppose in hindsight Patsy hoped I would change and accept her son and I hoped that she would seek an exorcism for them and relieve all of us of the curse which now dominated our lives. The answer to my problem came from an unexpected source.

"Clem!" George Nelson yelled at me. I released the trigger on my air chisel in order that I could hear what he had to say. "Clem I have been asked by the priest of that big Catholic church on the Pacific Highway if we did wood carving. He said the church had two large wooden support columns each side of the altar steps and could we do anything with them. I told him I would bring you along this afternoon to see what could be done."

"Sure thing George. In a way I miss working with wood."

"I told the priest that if we accept the job it would be on an hourly basis because you would have to do the work at the church. So when we look at the job I want you to estimate how long it would take, depending of course how elaborate he wants them carved."

"Sure. Once I have an inkling of his requirements I can give you a rough estimate of the time I would need." After our lunch break George drove the company flatbed truck out to the Pacific Highway. Seated on the passenger side amid dust and pieces of broken monuments, reminded me strongly of riding with my father in the old farm truck back in Gage County.

The priest waited for us in the church parking lot seated in a new Chrysler car.

"This is no poor parish Clem." George remarked. "Don't under-estimate the time you will need."

"This is my wood carver Clem." He said as we greeted the priest.

"Come into the church gentlemen and I will show you what I have in mind." He unlocked the huge door with a large black iron key and swung it wide for us to enter. He led us down the aisle to where a pair of eight inch square posts came up from the floor supporting a crossbeam high up near the ceiling. I saw immediately that I could turn one of the posts onto a giant crucifixion scene by adding a cross arm to the post similar to what I had done in the penitentiary. On the other I could create a roman soldier offering a vinegar soaked sponge to the Christ on a spear.

I had brought my portfolio of pictures from the prison and I showed the priest my work.

"Marvelous!" He declared.

Then I told him about my idea.

"You are suggesting a much bigger project than I had anticipated, Clem but I must admit I am impressed by your idea. I will of course have to run it by the parish committee but that is a hurdle I think I can clear, depending of course on the final cost. How many work hours do you feel it will take to complete?"

"A very rough estimate would be around five hundred, possibly less depending on how hard the wood has dried. I think the best thing would be for me to do some drawings then Mr. Nelson can give you a better estimate."

"Then let's meet here at the same time next week gentlemen, by then I will have met with the parish committee." As we parted at the church door I asked,

"Do you do exorcisms?"

"Good gracious no young man that is beyond my capabilities, why do you ask?"

"Just curious." I replied.

"Can you do the job in five hundred hours Clem?" George asked as we drove back to the monument yard.

"If I can adapt my woodworking chisels to the air tool it will be a piece of cake, but working by hand with a mallet it could be five hundred and more." The idea of working alone in the church gave me the seed of an idea how I could rid the world of John, without becoming a suspect.

George had been right, the parish had no cash flow problems and we were awarded the carving job at five hundred hours at George Nelson's rates, with me to receive a handsome bonus from him for on time completion. The following Monday we moved in scaffolding, a small compressor to run my adapted tools and lumber for the cross arm.

I began work immediately, not only on the carving job, but on my idea of saving my family from damnation by killing the boy. I established a routine of starting work at eight each morning and cleaning up the wood cuttings and dust at six each evening Monday to Friday and until noon on Saturday, when the church ladies came in to prepare the church for Sunday services. I had been on the job for three weeks establishing my routine. The situation at home had not improved. Patsy seemed to pretend that I wasn't there, avoiding speaking or any physical contact with me. I tolerated her behavior believing she would come around once the boys influence over her was ended.

I chose the Friday of the fourth week to execute my plan, for the priest usually dropped by at five in the evening to view my progress. At two thirty I drove to a street close to the school, parked, then went to the school gate and waited for John to come out.

"I've come to take you to see the carving I have been doing, the car is just round the corner." He just looked at me and obediently followed. I parked the car under some shade trees at the rear of the church parking lot where we both got out, carrying my two pound ball peen hammer. I looked around carefully to be sure I was not being observed. I stepped up behind John and drove the hammer head deep into his skull. He went down without a whimper. I felt an odd sense of deep excitement in my chest. I developed a strange taste in my mouth, my body shivered with a feeling of ecstasy similar to the final moments of lovemaking.

After ascertaining he had died, I stuffed his body into a gunny sack I had previously prepared with lots of sawdust and shavings in it to soak up any spilled blood. I placed the sack in the car trunk and with my heart beating wildly went back into the church to continue carving. Working the wood calmed me down and soon I felt elated that I had struck a blow for good against evil.

The priest came by as usual at around five and saw the pile of wood waste on the floor and admired my progress. He would be my alibi that I had worked all day in the church. I left the job at my regular time and drove home. The usually silent Patsy exclaimed,

"I'm worried about John. He hasn't come home from school and the child minder says he never showed up there this afternoon."

My first thought was that Patsy had begun speaking with me and I knew instantly that by killing the boy I had released her of at least part of the Branson curse. It occurred to me also, that the atmosphere in the house had been similar to the situation at the Branson bean farm between my parents when I was young. Now perhaps things would improve between Patsy and I and we could become young lovers again.

"Perhaps he is playing with a schoolmate and has forgotten all about the time. I'm sure he will show up soon."

"But this is so unlike John. He has never done this before. He has always told me if he might be late coming home."

"If he hasn't arrived home after dinner Patsy, I will take the car and look round the streets for him."

I ate the meal she had prepared but Patsy did not eat anything. I could tell that she was really worried. Frankly it didn't surprise me for I knew it might take some time before she realized that the boy's disappearance was a blessing I had bestowed upon her with love.

"I'm going out to look for him now Patsy. You stay here in case I miss him and he comes home. Don't worry my love it will turn out all right." Patsy looked at me oddly at hearing the words 'my love' for I had not uttered such things for quite a while.

I drove over the Golden Gate Bridge to the far shore

where I knew there was a trail leading down to the water's edge. I gathered a few heavy rocks and sat down to await the fast approaching darkness. When I felt the night would cover my activities I took the sack containing John, added the rocks, tied the top and hurled it into the fast out-flowing tide.

"I haven't been able to spot him anywhere Patsy. Is he home yet!" I yelled as I walked in. It was obvious that Patsy had been crying. It disturbed me somewhat. Maybe the curse would take longer to go away than I thought.

"Its past nine now Clem I think we should call the San Francisco police to report him missing."

"I think that may be a little premature Patsy, it is possible that he is at the home of one of his friends and had supper with them and is playing, oblivious to the time." However Patsy was adamant, she called the police and an officer named Richardson came round to ask for more information.

"He has never done this before officer. He would always let me know if he was going to be late."

"This happens more often than you would think Mrs. Branson. Sometimes children do silly things to get attention. More often than not it is the wrong thing and gets the incorrect result. If you can give me a photograph of John and a general description, we will have our officers' keep an eye out for him. If he hasn't shown up or contacted you by morning we will file a missing child report."

Patsy refused to try and rest. She paced the floor occasionally bursting into tears. The noise she made kept me awake. To be honest with you, her behavior annoyed me. I had broken the curse and yet she acted as though it still affected her. Her evil child had been saved from a life of spreading hate and unhappiness and the strong tide flowing from San Francisco bay was taking him far away from us.

At seven the next morning I readied myself for work but Patsy stated she was staying at home in case there was any news. I worked light heartedly while carving at the church; I felt I had done a great thing. I knew that before long Patsy would realize that she had been freed of Jed Branson's influence upon her and we could soon resume the joyous life we had together before the rape.

I arrived home to find the same policeman who had called last night.

"We still have no idea of the whereabouts of your son Mr. Branson. Apparently he left the school at the regular time and it seems he just disappeared. None of his classmates have seen him. After more than twenty-four hours it is beginning to look like he has been abducted."

"What does that mean?" I asked.

"It means Mr. Branson that someone may have lured the boy and taken him away. We cannot be sure of course but at this point it seems highly likely."

"Why would someone do that and where would they take him?" I asked expressing surprise and innocence.

"I'd really not like to go into detail at this time Mr. Branson. Suffice it to say that there are some strange and twisted characters out there. Just as a matter of interest where were you at three yesterday afternoon?"

"Are you suggesting that I had something to do with John's disappearance?"

No. But you must realize that we must investigate every aspect of the case and Mrs. Branson has told me that you and the boy were not on the best of terms. So where were you at three pm?"

"I am doing a carving job at the big church on the Pacific Highway I was there all day until I came home at around six, that's when Patsy told me he hadn't come home. In fact the priest came along to check my progress about three yesterday. He can vouch for my presence there at that time."

"Do you work alone at this carving job Mr. Branson?"

"Yes why?" He didn't answer but asked,

"Why did you and the boy not get along Mr. Branson?" I hadn't expected to be asked such a question and I was not really sure how to answer. I had to think carefully not wishing to give away too much of my history.

"It was just a father-son kind of thing officer. You know where kids like to push parental boundaries and I suppose I reacted to it."

"Did you ever strike the boy Mr. Branson?"

"No never."

"Do you have any relatives the boy may have run away to?'

"No. Neither Patsy or I have any living relatives." I saw Patsy looking at me for she knew I had murdered the last known one on my side. I thought for a moment she would tell the officer of my past and that I had recently been released from prison, but she remained silent.

"Have you any close friends the boy might have trusted and sought temporary refuge from your parental edicts, Mr. Branson?"

"No. Even if we had, they would have told us he was there with them."

"Is there anyone else the boy might have gone to stay with, perhaps a school friend he was particularly fond of?"

"I don't believe so, but then the same thing would apply. Surely they would not let us worry and wonder where he was."

"Of course not Mr. Branson, thank you for your co-operation. Let me assure you the department will leave no stone unturned until we find the boy."

The policeman left the house leaving Patsy and I alone.

CHAPTER NINE.

The policeman's final statement didn't worry me in the least, I knew no matter how many stones they turned over I knew they would not find the boy's evil carcass. Patsy began another crying session; frankly it surprised me for I thought that by now the curse would have been losing its strength. My first instinct was to berate her for tears shed for the malevolent child, but I quickly reasoned that she might need more time to adjust to his absence. Even though I had relieved her of the Branson curse, she might take some time to heal from the internal conflicts that had dwelt within her until now.

"Is there a dinner ready?" I asked.

"How can you think of eating when our son is missing?"

"Our Son!" I exclaimed in instant anger. "He is not my son Patsy. He is yours and my father's son! I did not know of his existence until recently so don't ever call him my son ever again!"

"You are my husband Clem and John is my son. As

far as I'm concerned to all intents and purposes and to the world in general, you are his father. You do not appear to be even remotely concerned for his well being Clem Branson. Neither do you seem to have any understanding about how I feel about John's disappearance. Prison has turned you into a cold fish, a man without feelings. You have become just like your own father, cruel, bitter and self centered. The only difference between the two of you is you do not have your father's insane religious ideas."

"How dare you even think of me in the same way as my father? He was a madman pure and simple. So far as I can figure out, so were most of his family. But by being drafted into the army I escaped the madness and broke the circle. Sadly he brought you and his illegitimate son right into it Patsy. Can't you see the boy and indeed yourself, carry his demented ideas?"

"What! Now I know you are just as crazy as he. I'll tell you this Clem, I have a feeling you know more about John's disappearance than you are letting on, to me or the police."

"Such an accusation on your part Patsy convinces me without a shadow of a doubt that my father's evil dwells within you. I know nothing more of the boy's disappearance than I have told you already!" By this time our discussion had turned to loud shouting and the argument was disrupted by the landlady at the door.

"Mrs. Branson!" She shouted at us. "I told you when you moved in here that I did not want any undue noise. Since your husband has joined you, without my permission I might add. The noise level has become intolerable. I want you out of here at the end of the month. No excuses, I want you gone on the thirtieth."

"See what you have done now." Patsy seethed. "As if I don't have troubles enough, I want you out of here now Clem. You have made it abundantly clear what you think of me and my son. No longer can I count on you for anything. It is just as it was when you first went to prison. One more time you have placed me in a position of rearranging my life as a result of your insane thinking and actions. Gather your things and get the Hell out of here and out of my life."

"You are the one who is insane Patsy. My father infected you with the Branson curse you don't seem to be able to escape it any more than the boy could."

"Could! Could! So you do know more than you are letting on! What have you done with my son? Where is he?" Have you harmed him?"

It was obvious that Patsy now suspected me in the boy's disappearance. I knew that if she told the police of her suspicions and my criminal record, the spotlight would be on me. The pressure might become too hard for me to deal with and I realized that I had to come up with a plan to get the heat off myself.

It was painfully apparent to me that Patsy would never be able to escape the circle of evil she was unknowingly in. Therefore it was up to me to help her. If the Branson curse was to be broken and destroyed for ever, Patsy had to pay the ultimate price. Loving her as I did, I knew the most loving act I could do for her would be to end her life.

"Very well Patsy, if you wish me to leave, I will." I said in a calm quiet voice. "Please let me know if there is any news of John. I will let you know where I am staying." I gathered up my clothes and walked out of the

194

house. I threw my belongings into the rear seat of my car and drove away. I knew I had to cover my butt until the time I killed Patsy, so I drove to the police department and asked for the officer who had been at the house. I told him,

"Due to the stress my wife Patsy is going through as a result of our son's disappearance she has asked me to move out of the house. I felt that I should stay to give her emotional support but she was adamant that I leave. Her imagination is playing tricks on her in her distress, so rather than add to her condition, I will be staying at the Regis hotel until the boy is found."

"Thank you for coming in and letting us know Mr. Branson. We understand how stressful this kind of event can be on parents. We will be in touch."

It occurred to me that in a way it was fortuitous that we had been asked to vacate the suite. For when Patsy moved out at month end it would not seem unnatural for a single tenant to have no forwarding address and become lost to her acquaintances, so this would be the time I would set her free.

I made a point of staying completely away for the next two days. Then I called at the apartment to see if she had heard any news of the boy. Patsy was as cold as ice with me and looked into my face with hatred in her eyes. I knew upon seeing her that way that the curse was gaining an even greater grip on her. There now was no doubt in my mind that she had to be relieved of the curse, the only way I knew how.

"Thanks to you and your ranting Clem Branson I have to move out of here in a couple of weeks. Fortunately I have found a smaller place closer to work and I can move in on the thirtieth."

"Then at least allow me to help you move your things for you with the car Patsy. It's the least I can do under the circumstances. I will also let the police know your new address in case there is any news of John being found."

Over the time she had been living in the suite, Patsy had amassed more belongings than she could carry on the bus, so she agreed I could help her to move. On the twenty eighth I went to the apartment on king road that she had rented.

"Mrs. Branson will not be able to move in as planned. She sends her regrets and an extra month's rent for your inconvenience." I told the landlady. I paid the extra rent, and then I went down to the police department and gave them a fictitious address where they could contact her if there were any new developments after the thirtieth. Next I removed the door handles and window winders from the car, with the exception of the driver's door. I removed the rear seats to make enough room for her goods and clothing. Now I was ready for the move and for my dear Patsy's release from the Branson curse.

I once again found the odd taste in my mouth in anticipation of my act of love for her. My heart beat much faster than usual and I found it difficult to concentrate on my carving work. At last the evening of the move came and I went to pick up Patsy and her belongings. She greeted me with a surly look which reminded my of my father and the way he looked at me. I knew without any doubt that my father's evil spirit lived within my dear Patsy.

"I have taken out the seats to make more room for your stuff." I told her. We loaded up the trunk then filled the back seat right to the roof with cartons and bags. I noted she had packed the boy's things, but I kept silent feeling this not to be the time for an argument.

"There are about five boxes left in the kitchen."

"I'll come back later for them when we have put this load in your new place Patsy." I said in a calm voice. I opened the passenger door and she climbed in, unaware that she could not get out of the car without my assistance or wind down the window to yell for attention. Patsy paid no mind to where I drove until she saw we were approaching the Golden Gate Bridge.

"Where the Hell are you going Clem? This is not the way to my new place!"

"I'm going to set you free Patsy" I smiled at her.

"Set me free from what." She demanded.

"I am going to free you from the Branson curse Patsy, just as I have freed your accursed son."

"What do you mean? What did you do to John?"

"It really doesn't matter Patsy, he is free now and so will you be very soon." I saw her reach for the door handle, but of course it wasn't there.

I watched panic rising in her and she began to scream. Her screams excited me, it felt similar to when I had dispatched the boy, I had the same odd taste in my mouth but now the taste and feeling was much more intense. She looked round but there was no escape from the rear for it was filled with boxes. I turned the car onto a deserted road several miles north of the bridge while Patsy continued to scream becoming even more panicked. I glanced at her face. She no longer bore the face of my beloved Patsy; it had become the sour miserable face of my father. If my mind had ever had a shred of doubt, it now cast it aside. He had completely taken her over. Evening shadows lengthened as I parked the car by some scrubby wind tortured trees.

"I am going to set you free now Patsy." I shouted over her screams. I felt for my hammer on the floor beside my seat. Upon seeing it she turned into a seething mass of utter fury and struck a stream of constant blows upon my face and chest with her hands and arms. I could not get a clear strike to her head so I guided the hammer full force upon her left knee. Her screaming stopped as she gasped in pain and put her hands on her injury. Now I had a chance to strike her head. I swung my hammer as hard as I could in the confined space and hit her on the temple. Patsy stopped moving. I opened my door and went round the car swinging open the passenger door. Patsy still breathed, so I pulled her out, laid her on the ground then reduced her head to a pulp with the hammer.

My body trembled with excitement. With my act of love I had freed her. As I gazed down at the lifeless but still twitching body, I knew that I had finally killed my father's evil spirit. It was his face staring sightlessly up at me and I remembered never having seen my father smile.

I retrieved the knife I had placed under my seat and cut her throat. I bled her like my father had bled the pigs back home on the farm. I sat, watched and waited until her thickening blood had drained into the dry soil. I felt intense pride in my actions. My Patsy would no longer have to suffer from the Branson curse. By my act of love for her I had eliminated it from the world; no one ever again would be affected by it.

I wrapped her head and neck in a bed sheet from a carton in the back seat then I placed her back in the passenger seat and drove to the high cliffs over the ocean on Route One. At a place where I could drive the car right up to the cliff edge I hurled Patsy's body over. There was no sound as she bounced upon a ledge then disappeared from my view. I emptied the car then threw all her belongings down into the ocean, followed by my hammer and knife. There was no blood in the car and no other evidence to link me to her demise.

I had a wonderful sense of elation. It was a feeling tantamount to the one I had when my army buddies took me to get laid for the very first time. Killing Patsy had left me in an odd kind of afterglow. I had no feelings of regret or fear of getting caught. Looking back on it now I think I had a spiritual experience, for I felt cleansed of all abuse and misery that had dogged me all of my life.

I stood on the cliff edge staring at the fog bank rolling in from the ocean toward the shore; soon the scene of my actions would be shrouded in heavy mist. I had a distinct feeling that God was giving me a clean worksheet to begin my life afresh, for my part in ridding the world of the evil I had been embroiled in. I sank to my knees and recited the prayers that had been drummed into me as a boy and had not repeated since the day I left Gage County to serve my country.

Darkness had fallen when I finished praying. I started the car and drove back to the hotel in San Francisco. I replaced the seats, door handles and window winders before going to my room. I did not sleep well that night, my mind and body were still in a state of heightened excitement. In the morning I returned to the church to continue the carving job. At this point it was about eighty percent complete; I knew that four or five days work would complete it. The priest was ecstatic about the results of my work and complemented me profusely. I felt a new sense of reverence working in the church as a result of my spiritual experience on the cliff top.

I was engaged in doing the final touches and sanding down the rough spots when the policeman who had been at the house walked into the church.

"Mr. Branson. I have been to your wife's last address. The landlady informed me that she had moved to a different apartment after asking her to leave. It seems that the two of you fought quite a bit and made lots of noise. Believe me Mr. Branson I know there is a great deal of stress when a child goes missing, however I do find it rather odd that Mrs. Branson would not have stayed in contact with my department just in case we came up with any leads. Do you have a forwarding address for her?"

"No I don't. Yes. We did argue about a number of things and so decided to separate. With the boy gone there was nothing to bind us together anymore. I have been living in the hotel as I'm sure you already know."

"Yes we are aware that you have spent every night there since before Mrs. Branson moved away. However the landlady at the old address seems to think that you helped her to move her things in your car. Can you tell me Mr. Branson, where you moved her belongings and where did you drop off Mrs. Branson?" I had to think fast for a satisfactory answer.

"I dropped her of at the bus station. She said she was going to New York as she couldn't bear to live here in San Francisco after what had happened to the boy. She took just two suitcases with her and the other belongings I got rid of in one of those big dumpster things in an alley in Chinatown."

"Can you recall which alley and block it was in Mr. Branson?"

"No. I just drove around until I found one that had just been emptied."

"Thank you Mr. Branson. If your wife does contact you please let us know. These missing children cases rarely close and it is important we have a contact in case of a break in the investigation." My answer seemed to have satisfied the officer and he left the church. I finished off the final touches on the project, swept the floor and left to go to the monument company.

"The job's all done boss." I called out to him over the noise of his air chisel.

"That's great Clem! The last time I talked to the priest he was very pleased with your work and so am I. It could be that we can branch out into doing more of this kind of work when the word gets around. There will be a nice bonus in your next pay envelope. Go and take the rest of the day off Clem, you have earned it."

I went back to my hotel, cleaned up, changed my clothes and went out for a drive. I toured along the pacific shoreline, and then stopped for a burger and coke in one of those roadside drive in's where you get your food at an outside window. I sat in the car eating my burger when a woman came to my driver's side window. She was dressed sort of provocatively and she reminded me of the girls my army friends and I used to meet when we were on furlough. She leaned into my window to speak, with her bosoms just about falling out of her blouse.

"Interested in a date? For twenty five I can show you a real good time." I just about choked on my burger. Her proposition was the last thing I had expected. By the time I had chewed and swallowed, I had made up my mind. It had been a while since Patsy and I had been together that way and her breasts were just about in my face through the open car window.

I nodded and she came around and climbed into the passenger seat.

"It's twenty five. My place or wherever you want." I leaned forward and got out my wallet to check if I had enough money. I pulled out a five and a twenty and showed it to her.

"I'm Clem. Your place is fine with me."

I'm Mandy. Go around the corner and into the alley I have a basement suite where we can be private. It's in that brown house second from the end." I parked and followed her through the door into a dingy ill kept room. A torn sofa stood against one wall, a kitchen table with two decrepit chairs against another and against the third an unmade double bed with sheets that had not seen a laundering for months.

I placed my twenty five dollars on the table and Mandy began to strip. I did likewise. As I joined her on the bed, I had the same strange and unusual taste in my mouth that I had experienced when I dispatched Patsy and the boy. I looked at her made up face. It had changed. Wrinkles began to form. Her eyes became beady and rat like. Her nose seemed sharper and her painted lips narrowed. My heart stopped beating for a few moments. This person had become my father. I knew instantly that he had come from the spirit world in the form of this

Mandy woman, in order to infect me with the Brandon curse.

I would not allow my father to get the best of me. I knew what I must do. I sat astride her then gripped her throat with both hands. I pressed my thumbs deep into her flesh and held on as she fought to get me off. She scratched me with her long nails, her legs flailing uselessly in the air. The taste in my mouth became more pronounced and sweeter as her struggles weakened. Her eyes were wide and glassy when she finally stopped moving, just the way my father's had been on the day I put him away on the farm kitchen floor.

I felt good. I knew I had triumphed over evil. I dressed and drew the soiled sheets over her body and head. I went to the door and looked around. I saw no one, so I went to my car and left the area. Once again I felt a strong warm feeling of afterglow despite the fact that sex had not occurred. I checked the San Francisco papers daily to see if anyone had found the body. Ten day's later the Chronicle reported that the upstairs tenant had reported a foul smell and the police had discovered a rotting corpse in the basement of the house. In their statement to the press, they said so far as they were concerned they could not come up with a motive for the killing. The woman was a known prostitute in the area and the money from her last client remained on the apartment table, eliminating robbery or theft. It was not as if I felt sorry for the dead woman. I didn't. She meant nothing to me; she had been possessed by the spirit of my dead father and as such in my opinion did not deserve to live.

On payday I received a sizable bonus and I decided

I would get a newer car, so I traded in my old Dodge for a 1951 Chevrolet two door sedan and I moved out of the hotel into a bachelor apartment not too far away from my job at the monument company. On reporting for work George Nelson said,

"You did a great job at the church Clem. The priest came round yesterday afternoon to pay the bill and he had nothing but praise for your work. I have a feeling that when he spreads the word around the diocese we can expect more jobs especially at the prices we charge."

"Thanks for the words of praise George. I have always enjoyed working with wood."

"Well Clem you will have to be content to work with granite and marble, until we get another contract with wood. I have nothing really spectacular for you to work on at the moment, just the run of the mill headstones."

My artistic abilities had no chance to shine doing the mundane work of preparing blank headstones, except for the occasional one requiring service club insignia or some other special touch for clients with a limited budget. I had lots of time for my mind to wander at will. It often took me to that special and most unusual feeling and taste in my mouth that had occurred when I had ended the life of those deserving of it. In an odd and strange way it reminded me of the glorious feeling I had shared with Patsy when she and I were first married. I remembered it as a total rush of the senses, a losing of one's self in the act and ending in an extraordinary feeling of afterglow, lasting unabated for hours.

I knew I had no desire to look for another woman to marry; there could never be another like Patsy. Yet over time, loneliness began to creep into my life. I had discovered that my creative side kept me in a happy frame of mind, but the routine and mundane stone carving left me with something missing from my life. My evenings were spent alone in my apartment sometimes reading, at others whittling chunks of hardwood into the likeness of a bird or animal.

It occurred to me that this was how I had spent my childhood. The only thing different, there was no stove with my father sitting beside it spitting into the flames and reading his bible out loud. The sudden realization that I was essentially regressing back to my childhood scared me. I wondered if my father's malevolent spirit was in the process of steering me back so that he could control my life again. The more I thought about it, the more plausible it seemed. I concluded that he had always controlled me. Even the killing of him in the farm kitchen had not stopped his control. Was not his act responsible for getting me put into prison, resulting in others controlling me for him? Did not his influence with Patsy and the beast of a son he had spawned, also exercise his control over me through them? Even the killing of all three had not stopped the circle of evil from surrounding me.

Now I was positive that it was his aim somehow to ruin my life and enslave me into the Branson circle of malevolence. What I did not know, was how to combat his evil influence? How could I fight an evil spirit? My father had always claimed he used prayer to ward off wickedness, but in retrospect it hadn't worked for him, as he was the very essence of malice. I wondered if my father was a black angel of Satan, but believing he was a white angel of God wandered the world causing misery to those whose lives he had touched in another time. I considered had he been recruited into the dark forces by his ancestors, for there appeared to be plenty of evidence pointing to that? Generations of the Branson's had the same penchant for cruelty and had passed it down like a congenital disease. Father had often ranted about the forces of evil; perhaps he had first hand knowledge of it?

I knew I had to spend less time alone in the apartment. I began taking in movies, while it took my mind off my loneliness for a short while, it always returned. On Friday and Saturday evenings I began going to bars not having to go to work the next morning and face George Nelson's ire. In a bar one Friday night I met a few guys who had served in Korea at the same time I did and found we had a fair amount in common. Some were still single, while others had marriages that had failed.

We all agreed the war over there had negatively affected us in one way or another. Some said the experience had hardened them to simple human feeling and were unable to feel close with the opposite sex. Still others felt a sense of anger that would not go away and tended to violently turn on anyone that annoyed them. Some felt our government had misled them and no longer had any faith in Washington affairs, while there were others who had been severely traumatized by the carnage and brutality of war and could relate to no one and drowned their feelings in alcohol.

I tried to analyze my own feelings about it. I saw things differently than my friends. For me my time in the service was an introduction to freedom. Freedom from my father, freedom to be my own man and freedom to excel as a supply truck driver. In my mind the fact that I had been wounded did not mean too terribly much, for it too gave me the freedom to come back stateside and meet with Patsy. My personal trauma began when I took Patsy to live on the Branson bean farm. I won't go into detail for I have already told you all about what happened there.

My new friends and I sat chugging back beer and reliving the Korean War all over again. I had trouble concentrating. My mind kept taking me back to that awful day when my father raped and infected Patsy with the Branson curse and impregnated her with his evil seed. As we consumed more beer my blood pressure began to elevate. The more I thought about that day and the results of it, the angrier I became. Several beers later Kirk Watson said.

"Who wants to come with me to find a couple of willing broads?" Thinking such a rendezvous would perhaps calm me down I said in a slurred voice,

"I'll go with you Kirk. Do you know where to find them?"

"Yeah Follow me." Together we staggered down a few streets on the edge of Chinatown. On an ill lit street several women leaned against the buildings,

"Looking for a good time boys?" one asked.

"Yeah." Kirk replied. Suddenly there were two women, one grabbed my arm and began leading me into a dark industrial door way.

"Twenty five and we can do it right here." I fumbled for my wallet and opened it. In the dim light figured I had got out twenty five dollars. She grabbed it from my hand and tried to leave. She was trying to rip me off, no doubt figuring I was too drunk to know the difference.

The anger that had been with me for hours burst from me in a blur of violence. I saw my father before me and I lashed out. I knocked her down with the second blow then grabbed her hair and began to pound her head onto the concrete. After about the fifth time hitting her head she ceased screaming. The odd but pleasant taste I had experienced before came to my mouth and I now knew what I had to do. I took my ever-present whittling knife from my pocket and stabbed her over and over again. I knew was killing my father for the second time. Blood trickled out of the doorway into the light. So I sat the body up in a corner and walked away.

I was sober now. I knew I had blood on my hands and clothing so I did not try to locate Kirk. I walked in shadows all the way back to my apartment and got inside without being observed. I cleaned myself up and put my clothes in a laundry bag intending to get rid of them in the morning. The wonderful feeling of afterglow enveloped me like a warm blanket and I slept like a newborn child.

I cooked myself a hearty breakfast of sausage and eggs, then took my laundry bag out to my car and took a long ride north and east of the city. Out in the farm country I threw the laundry bag into a reed filled irrigation ditch. The chances of some one finding it were miniscule and the chance of the clothes inside being connected to a San Francisco murder were completely remote.

I had no pangs of conscience about the killing the fact is, I had enjoyed it. The warm feeling when the deed was done felt wonderful. It reminded me strongly about the times Patsy and I were so close at the start of our marriage. Then the thought struck me! Perhaps Patsy's spirit was teaching me how to reward myself for setting her and the boy free from the Branson curse. Suddenly it all seemed to make sense! Her gratitude toward me was causing her to find a new way to please me and I felt it to be my duty to accept the pleasure and please her in return.

I drove back to the city with a completely new frame of mind. The love Patsy and I had shared lived on, albeit in a different form. I stopped at a corner grocery to pick up a paper and a case of coca cola. On the front page of the paper a large photograph showed the dead woman still propped up in a corner with dried blood spread across the sidewalk. The headline read.

'SECOND KNOWN PROSTITUE SLAIN WITHIN TWO WEEKS.' 'Police are investigating but at this point they have no clues. The dead woman who cannot be named pending notification of next of kin, is known to the police. The victim was found still clutching the money from her last john, ruling out robbery as the motive for her slaying. Police would not say if they thought the two murders were connected.'

I smiled. Only Patsy and I knew that they were.

"Great news Clem." Gorge Nelson said when I arrived at work on Monday morning. " I have been asked to give a quote on carving in a church in Sausalito. The word is getting around of your expertise. I said we would be there about noon. I presume you are ok about traveling across the bridge everyday for a while?"

"No problem George I'm free to move around now that my wife has left me, I could always get a room over there until the job was finished."

"Sure, we can tack on the cost of your accommodation

onto the total bill; it would probably be cheaper for them than paying hourly travel time. I can make it a selling point."

We drove to Sausalito and parked outside a huge church. We were met by the pastor and the head of the church council. Inside were massive columns of native California redwood logs while they had a beauty all of their own; the columns were plain with no embellishments. Immediately I could see tremendous possibilities and with redwood being relatively a soft wood to work with, the carving work would be easy.

"I see the twelve apostles six on each side with a massive crucifix suspended by heavy chains from the two front pillars hanging directly over the altar." The pastor looked at me in amazement.

"Young man, you have a great feel for what we had hoped to achieve. What would be the approximate cost and the materials you would need?"

George broke into the conversation,

"We would need to study the estimated number of hours, the cost of two redwood logs to make the crucifix, plus the cost of chain and miscellaneous supplies. If what my artist suggests is approved, we can get back to you mid week with a cost estimate and we could start work as soon as you give us the go-ahead. We can save you money by having you supply accommodation for Clement so we would not have to charge travel time each day."

To make a long story short we did get the job and the pastor found me lodgings with a parishioner a Mrs. Baxter. The lady in her mid fifties took in lodgers to supplement her small widow's pension. She made breakfast and dinner for me and packed a noontime lunch. I began work on the crucifix out in the parking lot. With the timber laid out on sawhorses the work was much easier than working vertically. I was able to use a chain saw in the soft redwood and just do the finishing work with my air tools. I had it completed and ready to hang after the first week we brought in a small lifting machine to hold the sculpture up while we chained it to the pillars through big iron rings. The pastor looked at the work with awe.

"Magnificent!" Was all he could say. The work had me so captivated I worked at it all the hours I could, the only time I halted work was on Sundays when the services were held. After six weeks of intensive labor the job was completed and I returned to my apartment in the city. It had been a profitable venture for George Nelson's company and he presented me with a large bonus.

"Take a week off Clem. You have earned it." It seemed odd having nothing to do. From my earliest memory I had always been busy, both on the Branson bean farm and the military, even the penitentiary had plenty of things to occupy my hands and mind. I drove back to my apartment to find police officer Richardson at my door.

"I have bad news for you Mr. Branson. We believe we have located the body of Mrs. Branson."

"In New York! She has died in New York?"

"No Mr. Branson we do not believe she ever went out of the San Francisco area."

"What do you mean officer? She didn't get on the bus after all?"

"A crab fisher boat's crew reported they saw what they thought might be a body on a ledge about twenty

211

feet above the waterline down below highway one, north of the city. When our investigators rappelled down to the body, they discovered many of her personal items strewn down the cliff face. From those and my personal viewing of the deceased I was able to identify the body of your wife."

"But it can't be! She went to New York!"

"Mr. Branson so far as we can figure you were the last person to see her alive. Perhaps you can explain how or why she would have changed her mind at the bus depot and went out and got herself murdered."

"Murdered! Did you say she had been murdered?"

"I have to tell you Mr. Branson you have become a person of interest to the San Francisco police department. The fact that your son went missing in mysterious circumstances and your wife is found murdered, puts a whole new light on things. By your own admission you didn't get along well with your son or Mrs. Branson. By all accounts you were the last person to see her alive that is if you really did drop her at the bus station."

"I did drop her off. I figured she would be on the next Greyhound bus bound for New York."

"Perhaps you could tell me Mr. Branson why she would be taking a kettle, coffee pot and cutlery with her?"

"Probably because she didn't want to have to buy new ones."

"Mr. Branson. We found sufficient goods to fill at least a half-dozen cartons it makes no sense to us that she would pay extra luggage charges in order to save money by repurchasing the items in New York. Even if she changed her mind at the last minute, she would have to put the cartons in another vehicle to get out to the cliffs on Highway One. Again this makes no sense to us. As you can imagine this makes you the prime suspect in her demise."

"Are you charging me with killing Patsy?"

"No Mr. Branson. I do not have sufficient solid evidence to prove the case, but I was hoping you might be able to give us a few new leads."

The policeman left and I grinned to myself. I knew they had nothing they could pin on me I had made sure of that. It was just unfortunate that Patsy's body and her belongings hadn't made it all the way down the cliff to the ocean. Had they done so, the nosey cop wouldn't have come around asking questions. I had an odd feeling that Patsy was congratulating me for evading his inquiries. As the day progressed I felt that she wanted to reward me. By evening the feeling was quite strong and so I went down town to find the source of my reward.

It wasn't difficult; I found any number of hookers in the area I went to. I chose a prostitute who, to some degree resembled Patsy. She had the same color of hair and in the same style although her clothing was much more provocative than Patsy would have worn. We agreed on a price for her services and I followed her to her dingy hotel room. We actually had sex and then I reached down to the bedside where I had placed a short length of quarter inch rope. She had a look of total surprise when I thrust it round her neck and tightened it as hard as I could. Her eyes opened wide as she gasped for air. The harder I pressed on the rope the more she took on the look of my father's contorted face. She kicked and struggled but had not the strength to push me away.

Once again I tasted that sweet and indescribable flavor in my mouth and throat. It took very little time for her to be still and as I stared at her I found myself in the state of afterglow I have described earlier. Patsy had rewarded me just like I knew she would. I felt wonderful as I dressed and folded the rope returning it to my rear pants pocket. It was a good clean killing with no spilled blood, I was glad I had thought of using the rope. When I was quite sure the bitch was dead I slipped twenty five dollars between her fingers, threw the bed sheet over her and left, making sure no one saw me.

Two day's later the papers headlined,

Serial killer at large in San Francisco
A third known prostitute found murdered.
Body discovered holding the cash from
her last trick. Police believe it to be the
work of the same person.

I felt proud of myself. I with the help of Patsy's spirit was able to fool the entire San Francisco Police Department; they had no clue with whom the responsibility lay. Since I had time off work I drove down the Coast Road and spent my nights in small town motels. After getting as far as Los Angeles, I retraced my route in time to report for work the following Monday.

"The police were here wanting to talk to you while you were away Clem. You are not in trouble are you?" George Nelson asked.

"No I don't think so. It is probably about the abduction of my son. Did the police say if they had found who had taken him?"

"No. But they did ask me to tell you to call them when you got back from your holiday." I didn't bother calling the police officer, I felt I had nothing to say to him and I knew they had nothing on one me they could prove. I had just completed cooking my dinner that same evening when the policeman knocked on my apartment door.

"May I come in to talk with you Mr. Branson? There are a few things that I need clarified in my investigation."

"I'm just about to eat my dinner."

"I am a patient man Mr. Branson I can wait." He sat in a chair watching me as I had my meal. "You recently bought a newer car Mr. Branson do you like it?" I wondered where this question had come from, who had told him and why.

"Yes I traded my old Dodge in on a Chevrolet. Why do you ask?"

"Do you remember me saying you had become a person of interest Mr. Branson? Well as a person of interest we have come to know a good deal about you. Through a check with Motor Vehicles we located the Dodge you traded in. Our forensic lab found small spatters of blood on the passenger door panel matching your wife's blood type. Can you explain how they got there?"

"Perhaps she scratched herself one time while we were out for a drive."

"A scratch Mr. Branson would more likely lead to a drip on the seat or door panel, it would be unlikely to cause a spatter. I am asking you if you disposed of the car to eliminate any possible evidence against you."

"No! Don't be ridiculous I had just got a bonus for the carving job I did in the Pacific Highway church so

I bought a better car. Surely it is no crime to trade in an older model."

"No it isn't. But Mrs. Branson was last known to be in that older model Dodge when she went missing. From my point of view it looks odd. It is also odd that your son went missing not long before your wife did and even more odd that you did not seem to let his disappearance upset you. Why is this?"

"I told you. We didn't get along."

"It is a pretty weak argument you have Mr. Branson. I suggest you know much more about this than you let on." I noticed that the officer stared intently into my eyes no doubt looking for a crack in my story. While I still had confidence the man was stabbing in the dark, I had begun to feel nervous. "In your work as a carver of stone and wood Mr. Branson, do you use hammers and chisels?"

"Naturally. Although now I use an air powered chisel in the monument yard. Why do you ask?"

"On a secondary search of the cliff face, my men found a ball-peen hammer and a knife. The ball part of the hammer matched exactly the dents in Mrs. Branson's skull and the knife had traces of her blood on the blade and we believe the same knife was used to cut her throat before her body was hurled over the cliff. In addition so much of her personal belongings were cast over the edge it stretches the imagination to think that someone picked her up at the bus depot and took her and all those things to the murder site. The things that by your own admission had been in your car when you took her to the station. What is really odd Mr. Branson is that your initials are carved into the handle of the ball-peen hammer. Can you give me any logical reason why Mrs. Branson would have your hammer in her possession?"

"Perhaps she intended to use it when she got to New York to hang pictures and the like."

"It's a possibility, but a weak one. I suggest Mr. Branson that you hurled the hammer and knife along with your wife's body and her belongings over the cliff after you had killed her. Is this not so?"

"No I left her at the bus station like I said. Perhaps she was having an affair and lied to me about it. Maybe her lover picked her and her belongings up and killed her to get out of the relationship."

"Once again Mr. Branson your argument is weak. I am giving you the opportunity to tell me the truth of the matter. If you do, the state will go easier on you if you come clean."

"I have told you the truth. It is all a mystery to me why she ended up dead."

"Have it your way then Mr. Branson." Officer Richardson went to the door and opened it. A different policeman stepped inside.

"I am Detective Wade. I have a warrant to search your apartment Mr. Branson." It didn't worry me unduly for I knew there was nothing here to incriminate me.

"Go ahead there is nothing here to connect me to your theory." The two officers went through everything in the apartment and then left with a few articles in a paper bag without telling me what they were. I began to wish the police would leave me alone, after all they could not prove anything. I had been much too smart for them. I had just finished carving the words 'In Memoriam' on a headstone blank when George Nelson tapped me on the shoulder. I turned off my air chisel and turned to face him.

"There are two cops here to see you Clem. What the hell have you been up to?" Officer Richardson stepped up.

"Clement Branson, I am charging you on suspicion of the crime of murder." He read me my rights and I responded,

"You have the wrong person. I know nothing about my wife's murder I already told you that."

"Yes you did Mr. Branson. The fact is we don't believe you. You are required to accompany us downtown to the precinct office." I looked into Richardson's face. He had a hint of a smile as though he had just bested me. The look was one I was more than familiar with. It was the same twisted rat like expression my father had always used. I realized instantly that my father's spirit had taken Richardson over. There was only one thing I could do. I turned on the air chisel and lunged at him. The chisel point had dulled and it did not penetrate through his clothes. The other policeman dove at me and knocked me down. They had handcuffs on me in seconds as George Nelson looked on with a look of disbelief on his face as the police marched me to a waiting car.

Being held in a cell held no great trauma for me. I knew I would get out because they had no real evidence to keep me here. When they took me to an interview room I had forgotten they would charge me with the assault of a police officer and resisting arrest. My confidence began to wane

"In addition to the felony assault charge Branson, you are charged with the murder of Carol Sage."

"I know nothing of such a person. Once again you have made a big mistake."

"In a search of your apartment we found a length of rope with the hair of the victim entwined in it. The hair is an exact match to the victim's. Carol Sage is a prostitute known to us and she was found dead after sexual intercourse and strangulation. The woman was found clutching twenty five dollars in her hand two other prostitutes have been found dead with the same calling card. One, Mandy Coleridge was stabbed repeatedly with a whittling knife which we also found in your apartment, a second was found strangled with finger marks on her throat. We know we can convict you on these three murders and we believe you also murdered your wife and son given your record we are sure we can make those stick also."

"What do you mean my record?"

"We know you have murdered before Branson. You served ten years before being granted an early pardon for the killing of your father. It will be no stretch for a jury to convict you on the last five killings. Which brings us to the reason why you committed the crimes; can you tell us what motivated you?"

I didn't answer. I knew Richardson had been infected by the spirit of my father for it was his face staring at me across the interview table.

"It was then doctor that they sent me to you for Psychiatric evaluation. I have told you just about everything I can remember about my life. My one regret is that despite all my efforts I have not been able to break the Branson curse and circle of violence. I know that I broke free of it when I joined the army, but sadly the power of the curse lives on and my father is still able to pass it on to others just as his ancestors passed it onto him."

"I appreciate your candor Mr. Branson; I will pass my findings on to the court on the day of your trial."

"Thank you doctor. What do you think will happen to me, will I they send me to Alcatraz Island?"

"I have no control over what the court will or might not do Mr. Branson. The decision as to your future is in their hands, but I will present my findings to the court as fair and honest as I can. Good luck Mr. Branson."

On the day of my trial I pleaded not guilty on the advice of the state appointed lawyer. The psychiatrist told the court that he thought I was delusional and mentally unbalanced as a result of my father's treatment of me as a child. He said it was his opinion that I was unfit to stand trial and that I should be incarcerated into the state institution for the criminally insane. The judge agreed with him and so I am in here for the rest of my life. I have no regrets about being here. I know I released my beloved Patsy and her evil son from the Branson curse, for me that is all that matters.

Alan's interest in writing began at age seven when his teacher praised a five page composition on his summer adventures.

During his working years he gained insight into many different levels of society from Vancouver's sleazy Eastside, to boardrooms. Alan continued to write. He became west coast correspondent for his national company's quarterly magazine winning three awards for his contributions plus an award for adult fiction.

Upon his early retirement he began to write seriously, encouraged by the Penticton Writers and Publishers writers group.

This is his fifth novel. He also writes several genres of poetry, completed a large number of short stories and a book of humor. His poetry has been published in three countries and he performs his cowboy poetry at cowboy poetry festivals. He has had numerous articles published in the daily news press.

ISBN 142511317-6

9 781425 113179